# CLAIMING HER
## A REVERSE HAREM ROMANCE

## ANGELA SNYDER WRITING AS
## A.J. SNYDER

# COPYRIGHT

Copyright © 2018 Angela Snyder writing as A.J. Snyder
This book is a work of fiction. Names, characters, places and incidents either are products of the author's imagination or are used fictitiously.
All rights reserved. No part of this publication may be reproduced, stored in retrieval system, copied in any form or by any means, electronic, mechanical, photocopying, recording or otherwise transmitted without written permission from the publisher. You must not circulate this book in any format.
This book is licensed for your personal enjoyment only. This book may not be resold or given away to other people. If you would like to share this book with another person, please purchase an additional copy for each recipient. If you're reading this book and did not purchase it, or it was not purchased for your use only, then please return to the retailer and purchase your own copy. Thank you for respecting the hard work of this author.

## AUTHOR'S NOTE

*Claiming Her* is a reverse harem romance containing adult content for mature readers.

You can find all of my books exclusively on Amazon and free for Kindle Unlimited subscribers: http://amazon.com/author/angelasnyder

Please sign up for my newsletter to be notified of all of my new releases, giveaways, sneak peeks, freebies and more: http://eepurl.com/cNF0o5

# SYNOPSIS

The new flu vaccine that was supposed to save lives turned humans into bloodthirsty zombies instead.

For the past two years, Trinity Sanders has found herself fighting for her life in an apocalyptic world she never imagined would exist.

After she's suddenly caught in someone's trap, Trinity thinks her fate is sealed. However, when she wakes up in a strange house and in a warm bed, she's surrounded by other humans, not the ravenous monsters she was running from.

The four handsome men who saved her are rough, rugged…and wild. They've lived on their own since the apocalypse, surviving on the land and claiming whatever they capture in their traps, which now includes Trinity.

In a world with no rules, you claim what you want…

And they all want her.

*NOTE:* Claiming Her: A Reverse Harem Romance contains adult content for mature readers. It is a 40,000+ word standalone romance with a HEA.

# PLAYLIST

Lana Del Rey - *Gods and Monsters*
Metric - *Help I'm Alive*
Chvrches - *Never Say Die*
Bring Me the Horizon - *Sleepwalking*
Bad Wolves - *Zombie*
Falling In Reverse - *Alone*
Breaking Benjamin - *Torn in Two*
Red - *Let It Burn*

# PROLOGUE

*Trinity*

IT FEELS LIKE I'm in a dream that I desperately don't want to wake up from.

As I stare at the four rough, rugged and handsome men who have claimed me as theirs, I realize that I never even thought about a scenario such as this one in the world that existed before the apocalypse. But now, in the *new world*, I can't deny what I want.

What I need.

What I *crave*.

Lucas wraps his strong arms around me as we dance to a slow country song while Owen, Carter and Jack watch from a few feet away. Wrapping my hands around Lucas's neck, I pull him down to me, his lips meeting mine in a passionate kiss.

Like all the other times we kiss, the world around us begins to melt, and we are the only two that exist in our own little bubble.

And it isn't until I feel a warm body sliding up behind me that it hits me that we're not alone. Carter turns me so that my front is pressed up against him and my backside is pressed up against Lucas.

And then, he gently grips my chin and tilts my head up so that my lips meet his in a soul-searing kiss.

While Carter devours me, Lucas's hands roam all over my body, my breasts, my hips, my ass before cupping my cheeks hard and pulling me tight up against him. The evidence of his arousal pushes deep into my backside, and I gasp loudly.

Carter's lips move over my jaw and then to my neck, licking and biting gently as I throw my head back to rest on Lucas's chest.

With me sandwiched between them, they have their way with me, grinding their thickening lengths against me while their hands wander over my body.

Suddenly, Carter grabs the hem of my dress and tugs it up my thighs. And with Lucas's help, they pull it up over my head.

With no bra or panties on, I'm completely bared to them. But I don't feel exposed.

*I feel free.*

"Fuck, you're gorgeous," Carter whispers against my neck before he lightly nips at my skin and then soothes the bite with his talented tongue. His mouth moves lower, trailing down my neck to my breast where he sucks on my pebbled nipple, taking it into his warm mouth and sucking until I'm aching with need.

While Carter's attention is on my breasts, Lucas's adept fingers dip between my legs, finding my already wet seam. He groans against my hair as he slips a finger inside of me, pumping in and out so slowly.

"All of us want you tonight, Trinity," Lucas whispers into my ear. "But the question is…do you want all of us…all at the same time?"

I only hesitate a moment before I moan out a yes.

When Owen and Jack join the three of us, I feel overwhelmed, completely dominated…but I've never felt more alive, more turned on or more loved in my entire life than in this very moment…

# CHAPTER 1

*Trinity*

*2037*

IN 2032, THERE was a strain of the flu that wiped out a quarter of the world's population within the period of a few months.

As we all grieved for the loss of so many of our loved ones, the world around us began to undergo changes. People began to walk around with surgical masks on their faces twenty-four-seven. They became an obsessive-compulsive germaphobe overnight in the face of the epidemic, stocking up so heavily on Lysol wipes and hand sanitizer that stores couldn't even keep them on the shelves.

People eventually stopped shaking hands, going to grocery stores and malls, visiting friends and family, even going to church.

The economy was beginning to crumble right before our eyes, and the government demanded a solution.

And so, with so much pressure on the CDC to come up with some type of cure, a new universal vaccine was created hastily inside a lab in London. It was immediately dubbed the *miracle cure*, and it's all anyone talked about on the news or on the internet. This supposed cure-all was going to save the rest of our population and have the economy bouncing back.

But the trials were short. *Too short.* If it worked on rats, it should work on people, right? And since the rats didn't show any signs of abnormalities, the CDC deemed it suitable for us humans.

The universal vaccine was only given to a certain percentage of pharmacies in every city across the United States until more could be produced and shipped.

I hate to imagine what would have happened if they would have given the vaccine to everyone.

Because what came next would ultimately change the future of our planet and the people who reside on it. *Forever.*

Days after the new serum was distributed, the hospitals quickly became overrun with people who were showing atypical symptoms. At first, it appeared they had some new form of the flu or a bad allergic reaction to the vaccine.

They had trouble breathing. They suffered from internal bleeding and hemorrhaging as their organs began shutting down one by one. Their skin broke out in rashes and blisters, and it was as if the virus was eating them alive from the inside out.

A high-grade fever was the very last symptom, causing extensive brain damage and seizures, leading to unconsciousness and, ultimately, premature death.

And then, shortly after they were pronounced legally dead, they began to come back to life…with an appetite for unaffected flesh.

Yeah, the hospitals were the first to be overwhelmed with these creatures that everyone designated *zombies* overnight.

People barricaded themselves inside their houses, but the zombies were powerful and fast, destroying entire neighborhoods overnight. No place was safe, and the world quickly declined.

Businesses shut down. Churches closed their doors. Hospitals were boarded up and left vacant. There were no more supermarkets, malls, or convenience stores.

But the thing I remember the most is the day the lights went off and never came back on.

It's amazing how you take all the little things for granted.

Like lights.

Talking on the phone.

Going for a long drive with the windows down.

Picnics in the park.

*Music.*

God, sometimes I think I would actually kill someone just to hear my favorite songs again.

Eventually, the creatures began to slow down as their bodies began to deteriorate to the point they had trouble moving even in the undead state.

Once they began to slow, that's when my group made our first move to get out of the town we were holed up in. We had run out of everything, even basic supplies, and so our only choice was to run.

Running had never been a pastime or hobby of mine, or something that I even enjoyed, but I quickly learned that I would need to for the rest of my days on this god-forsaken planet.

A group of us, including my best friend, a couple of our co-workers from the elementary school we worked at and some strangers we picked up along the way ran from the city and hid in small towns where the epidemic hadn't hit quite as hard.

We learned quickly that the zombies were attracted to three things: movement, sound and light.

And so we lived in a world of stagnant and silent darkness.

It kept us alive for a while. We made it one month, then six…then a whole year.

But on the one-year anniversary since the world had turned upside down, I was awakened to the sound of screaming…

At first, it felt like I was stuck in a dream…or maybe more like watching a horror movie play out in front of my eyes.

We had been camping on the outskirts of a small town that had been overrun by zombies. We were taking turns keeping watch all night long, but obviously someone had messed up and fallen asleep.

The sun was just starting to crest over the mountain, illuminating the horrific sight before me.

My best friend, Joanie, the girl who I had known since the sixth grade, went to college with and worked with, was being attacked by one of those monsters.

And what did I do?

I fucking froze.

And then, I helplessly sat there and watched as the zombie ripped into the flesh in her neck, effectively silencing her screams.

Her big, brown eyes locked on mine, but I couldn't even move or blink. Tears filled my eyes, effectively blurring her and the zombie attacking her, as I stood and slowly backed away from the gruesome scene before me.

"I'm sorry," I whispered to her. "I'm so sorry."

*You fucking coward!* I screamed in my head. But Joanie was too far gone to save, and I would ultimately die in the end if I even tried to intervene now. I didn't even know I had survival instincts until the world turned to shit.

The rest of the group was already running away, and so I gave my best friend one last look before I held back my sobs and ran to catch up.

The next to die several months later was a guy named Javier. He had been tall, dark and handsome and married in the *old world*, as I began to refer to it as. In the *new world*, his face was ripped off by a flesh-eating monster and his wife had died over a year ago in a hospital shortly after receiving the flu vaccine.

One by one, our group was slowly picked off until we were down to three...

"WE GOTTA GO," Henry says suddenly, breaking me out of my reverie.

I give him a nod before hauling myself up from the riverbank where I had just gotten a drink of water.

Our group of three consisted of myself, Henry and Florence. Henry had been the vice principal at the school where I'd worked, and he took on the role as the leader of our small ragtag group after Javier died.

Florence, the former school secretary, and I simply follow him, hoping that Henry will somehow protect us, but knowing that when push comes to shove, he'll probably shrivel up and die along with the rest of us.

Javier had been a natural born leader, leading us to supplies and food easily. Henry keeps taking Florence and me in circles and leading us to danger that we have to escape from.

Henry takes a backpack from my hands and slips it onto his back. "I'll carry it this time."

I give him a small smile. "Thanks." Even though the bag is filled with meager supplies, it gets heavy after walking for so long with little to no nutrients in my body.

"Come on, Florence. It's been ten minutes," Henry says impatiently, checking his wristwatch again and counting every second we're wasting.

Florence is an older woman in her early sixties with short, curly, salt-and-pepper hair and kind eyes. However, her age is becoming a huge factor when her knees and hips constantly give her problems, causing us to take long pauses in our journeys across the state of Pennsylvania.

Stopping for long periods of time is simply not an option, and it makes Henry and I very skittish.

I watch as Florence tries to stand and falls back down on the ground. "I can't go on anymore," she says with tears tracking down her plump, sunburned cheeks. "Just…just leave me here."

Henry glances at me, his face full of optimism that I'll agree to leave her behind. But I quickly squash that idea. "No, no way. We all go or none of us go, remember?" I tell her, reciting the only rule we've had since the very beginning of this shit-show.

Henry's been getting really creepy and clingy as of late, especially after we lost Javier, and it's starting to freak me out a little. I need

Florence to stay with us, because I'm afraid of what Henry might do if Florence ever leaves.

I think we're all going mad at this point from dehydration and hunger, but Henry outwardly shows the symptoms more than the two of us combined.

"Fine," Henry huffs. He quickly walks over to an old log and breaks off a long, thick branch. "Use this as a cane. It might help," he says, handing the makeshift walking stick out to her.

Florence nods and grabs the wood in her hands, using it to put most of her weight onto as she finally stands. "Okay, okay," she whispers. "Let's keep going. It's going to be dark soon."

"Maybe we can find a car," I say, but even I can hear the doubt in my tone. Cars have become a precious commodity in this world. But even more precious than that? Fuel. We've stumbled upon a lot of vehicles abandoned on highways and roads like an apocalyptic junkyard, but we never find one that doesn't have an empty gas tank.

Yeah, instead of a car, we need to find shelter. Hell, we need to find way more than shelter. We need to find other humans, people who will take in some sad souls like us and offer some sort of protection. Maybe even food.

My stomach growls loudly at the thought of food, and I wrap my arms protectively around my waist. We managed to survive this past winter, and I thank my lucky stars that it was a mild one — probably the mildest we've ever had in Pennsylvania that I can remember. The winter before that was harsh, but at least we had been inside.

With spring in full swing, it's getting warmer; and finding food will become easier for us.

I haven't eaten in days, and I can feel my body trying to shut down.

I'm weak, but I keep walking, keep moving. It's the only way to stay safe.

At least when Javier was alive, he knew how to forage and catch fish. He kept us alive and our bellies full. The three of us left in the group don't know how to do any of that kind of stuff. Now, we've been surviving on the sparse rations we found two towns back.

As the three of us stroll through the woods, Henry comes up close to me and whispers into my ear, "Maybe in the next town we'll find some supplies. We can dump Florence and continue on. Just you and me. We can make a life for ourselves; create our own world, our own family."

His words have alarm bells going off inside my head. However, I force a calm demeanor on the outside, not letting him know that I absolutely abhor him and the idea of being stuck with him. I can't let on that he's freaking me out, or it might trigger whatever the hell is going on with him and maybe even make it worse.

Henry always did voice his attraction for me while he was my boss, but I always shot him down. There were rules in place back then, however. Out here, there are no rules. Not anymore.

I don't want it to be just him and me. *Ever.* And if I find people, a place to stay, I will never leave there. The best thing to do is to find a group of survivors and stick with them. Creating our own world is just crazy talk, and I refuse to give in to him…even if I am feeling a little crazed from hunger at this moment.

And so I continue walking, staying ahead of him and not saying a word.

But I'm tired of running. So damn tired. And just when I'm ready to suggest we take a break, a snapping twig nearby has me stopping dead in my tracks. "Wait!" I whisper-yell to the other two.

Everyone stops walking, and we just stand there. Listening. For something. *Anything.*

And then I hear it again over to the left. Something is moving through the woods, tracking us. It's getting dark, so it's hard to see, but I feel it in my gut that something is coming for us.

That's when the sound of a feral growl resounds through the woods, causing a cold shard to splinter inside of my spine and ice to flow through my veins.

"Run!" I gasp, taking off in the opposite direction of the sound.

I hear Henry and Florence's footsteps behind me for a while. But poor Florence is picked off before she even makes it a hundred feet. I can hear her piercing screams, but know I can't stop.

Stopping means pain.

Stopping means death.

*Every man for himself* really has a whole new meaning nowadays.

And there's absolutely no helping someone once they're caught by one of *them*. Their fate is already sealed the moment they're bitten.

I feel Henry flanking my right side, and so we just keep running like our lives depend on it. And they do.

The woods look like they end up ahead, and I can almost see a clearing with maybe a house or a barn in the distance. If we can just make it to the clearing, we might be able to find shelter or somewhere to hide.

I'm so focused on getting to the clearing that I completely miss the huge log that I ultimately trip over, causing me to crash to the forest floor. Twigs and pebbles cut into my hands and knees as I tumble. My forehead collides with a sharp rock, knocking me out for a few seconds.

When I come to, I sit up slowly. The world around me tilts on its axis before eventually righting itself. My head pounds with a ferocious headache, and I hiss out in agony. When I touch the source of the throbbing, blinding pain on my forehead, my fingers come back covered in blood. I shudder at the sight, my entire body trembling.

*They can smell blood.*

I hear the zombie's growls and know it's getting closer, but I can't seem to get my limbs to cooperate with my brain.

Henry was ahead of me, but he quickly ran back for me when he realized I wasn't following him. He leans down to me, his hand outstretched with a panicked look on his face. I reach for him and am thankful for the help up.

He roughly wraps his hand around my arm and propels me forward. With a bout of dizziness hitting me, his push almost sends me down again. I trip but manage to keep myself upright this time.

"Keep running, Trinity," he seethes. "It's right behind us!"

With a newfound panic, I burn the last of my energy as I make the clearing up ahead my destination. My thighs and legs are killing me, but I push forward, promising myself a long rest just as soon as we're safe.

My vision starts to blur and my head pounds like there's a jackhammer inside of my skull, but I'm determined to make it. I'm not going to give up now, not after everything I've survived and sacrificed up until this point.

The edge of the woods grows closer and closer, and I feel a sense of overwhelming relief flooding through my veins. Once we're out in the open, we will be able to see the threat way more easily. We'll escape. We'll be okay.

But I never make it.

One minute my feet are pounding against the leaves and twigs on the ground, and the next I'm being hauled up in the air, trapped inside a large cargo net.

The force of being flung upwards steals all the breath from my lungs, and it's a full minute before I'm able to suck air back into them.

"Trinity!" Henry yells.

My hands search around for a way out of the damn net, but the top is cinched too tightly. I peer out between the small openings in the net and spot Henry about twenty feet down below me. Even if I manage to get out of the net, I'll fall and probably break my legs or worse.

"Run, Henry! Run!" I hiss at him. I can hear the zombie coming closer, and the noise we've been making will only attract more. Henry will never make it if he doesn't run right now. "Run!"

And then he does. He leaves me there just like we left all the others before us that had their fate sealed at the hands of the creatures.

I curl up into a tight ball and keep quiet, barely breathing and thankful that I'm high up off the ground — too high for the zombie to reach.

I hear twigs snapping and what sounds like a foot dragging along the ground. Then, the zombie is below me, scratching at the bark on the tree and snarling like a feral animal. It can probably smell the blood from the wound on my forehead. Quickly, I clamp my sleeve and hands down on my head, praying silently for some kind of miracle.

Squeezing my eyes shut, I block out everything around me and reminisce about my life in the *old world.*

I had been happy with a career that I absolutely loved, teaching the fourth grade at the local elementary school. I busted my ass all through high school and then college, always knowing what my end goal was. I always wanted to be a teacher.

Even though I had my dream job, I didn't have a boyfriend or a husband or kids of my own. But that was always the next step. A happy family — something I never had the chance to experience in life.

I owned my own home, a cute two-story house in a good neighborhood with a playground across the street. I had been so proud the day the real estate agent put up the *sold* sign on the front lawn. It was a place I could call my own, a place my kids could call home. A stable environment, much unlike the place I grew up in.

My childhood hadn't been an easy one. I bounced around in the foster care system from the age of six after my drug-addicted mother decided she loved drugs more than her own daughter.

And who knew where my sperm donor of a father even was. Hell, my mother probably didn't even know his full name.

Maybe he died from the flu years ago. I would probably never find out.

Yeah, I thought I went through hell and back as a child…but I had no idea what I was going to experience later on in life.

Keeping my eyes tightly shut, I focus on breathing shallowly and evenly. And after a while, I no longer hear the zombie; just the soothing sounds of the forest and a river nearby.

Eventually, I allow the sounds to lull me into a deep sleep.

# CHAPTER 2

*Jack*

MY LIFE HAS become a monotonous routine. Get up, take a shower, brush my teeth, comb my hair, get dressed, eat breakfast, check the traps and hunt. Then, I come home, eat, shower and go to bed.

Every day it's the same damn thing.

But hell, it could be worse. *A lot worse.*

The world went to absolute shit almost two years ago, and things haven't gotten any better for most of the world's population. I'm one of the lucky ones I suppose.

I had been a Marine in what I consider now to be my old life. I was damn good at my job too, doing four tours in Iraq and saving fellow soldiers' lives too many times to count.

When push came to shove, I got the job done no matter the situation. And I think, in a lot of ways, it prepared me for the apocalypse that hit the world abruptly and rapidly.

I really put my skills to the test when I saved the small group of guys that I'm with now. We were all part of a much larger group, but most of them didn't make it. Sickness and disease took a lot of our group out, but we also ran into a lot of zombies.

The four of us traveled for a long time until we ended up at River's Edge Farm in upstate Pennsylvania.

The farm had everything we needed: a river with fresh water and plenty of fish, acres of open land, animals to supply food and eggs, a well, and a fence that ran the entire perimeter of the property.

We lucked upon the spot and couldn't believe our eyes that it had been abandoned. And just like that, River's Edge Farm became our new home.

We reinforced the fences, set up traps and whatnot to ensure our safety. And while we don't live in total comfort of not being attacked...or worse, the measures we took help us to sleep better at night.

As I walk through the woods, I creep quietly, trying not to kick up any rocks or break any twigs or branches. I've encountered too many of *them* out here that I've lost count. There are lots of words for the people who turned into monsters after getting that flu vaccine. Zombies or creatures are the more popular terms.

All I know is that they are creepy fuckers that I will kill without a moment's hesitation.

I never venture off the main property without a few knives, a gun and extra ammunition. I'm decked out in hunting gear that helps to keep me camouflaged from all creatures, and I'm doused in deer piss to throw off my scent to any of those zombie motherfuckers.

You can never be too careful.

My eyes sweep the area ahead of me as I walk. Every now and then I stop and do a full turn to survey my surroundings. I have an ear and a sixth sense for danger, but I don't always leave it to chance and gut feelings.

Things have changed now. Drastically.

As I approach a small trap, I see that it hasn't been set off, and so I leave it be. There have been weeks when I haven't caught a damn thing, and some days when I catch several small game. I hunt everything and anything, because me and my guys need to eat. We have to stay fed and strong, or we'll never survive this world.

When I reach my next destination, I stop dead in my tracks. My large cargo net has been tripped. And the only thing that can trip it is large game. I set the trigger to only go off for anything fifty pounds and over.

I stare at the net high up in the tree and notice a big bundle inside covered in the leaves and twigs that concealed the net on the ground. Whatever's inside is not moving, and I don't know whether that's a good thing or a bad thing.

Grabbing the rope by the tree, I slowly lower the net. When it gets to the last five feet or so, I let the rope go and allow the thing to fall to the ground with a thud.

The net spreads out, and I ready my gun as I stare at the unmoving object, waiting for something to happen.

But nothing does.

It looks like a baby bear cub or something, curled up in a brown mess of twigs, leaves and dirt.

I reach for one of my hunting knives and put my gun away. Leaning down to the creature, I hold my knife at ready as I start clearing away the debris.

A woman's bloody face appears, and I'm so taken aback that I fall back on my rear-end on the ground.

"Holy shit," I whisper to myself.

We haven't come across another human in a long time, let alone a *woman*.

Most of the women and children were, unfortunately, the first to die in the epidemic. My group of people that I escaped with only had one woman in it, and she died fairly early on.

The woman before me has a nasty gash on her forehead. Her long, dark hair is littered with debris from the forest, and she's covered in dirt from head to toe. No wonder I couldn't tell what the hell she was at first.

I slowly crawl over to her and check her pulse. It's faint, but it's there. That's all that matters.

Gathering her up in my strong arms, I stand and cradle her against my chest. Her head lolls against me, and it feels…*right*.

"All right, Sleeping Beauty. Let's get you home," I whisper to her as I leave the woods and venture back towards River's Edge Farm.

# CHAPTER 3

*Carter*

I'M JUST FINISHING up nailing and fixing a piece of fence when I see Jack coming back from his hunting trip. Glancing at my wristwatch, I realize he's early. And that's when I notice he's carrying something in his arms.

"Hell yeah," I mutter under my breath. We haven't had any large game in a while, and I'm hungry for some good deer meat. Eating fish every day is getting fucking old.

But the closer he gets, I see that it's not *something* he's carrying, but *someone*.

"Who the fuck is that?" I ask, when he's in hearing range, pointing my hammer towards whatever the hell he's got.

"A woman," he says nonchalantly, as if it's a totally common occurrence.

I cock a brow at him. "Where'd you find her?" I ask, curious as all get-out.

"In one of my traps." He looks down at the woman in his arms. I can't see much of her, not even her face since it's currently hidden against the big man's chest. "Go get Lucas," he tells me with a serious look on his face.

Not like he's never *not* serious, though.

I give him a nod and rush to the farmhouse. It's hard to believe this place has been our home for the past several months. I met up with Lucas, Jack and Owen in central Pennsylvania, and we somehow made it here in one piece. It's like a slice of fucking paradise in the middle of the world's complete and utter ruin.

Lucas is in the living room when I rush through the door. The look on my face must tell a picture worth a thousand words, because he doesn't even ask what's wrong, but instead bolts out the door, leaving me standing there.

I run out after him just as Jack is carrying the woman through the front yard with Owen, the fourth man of our group, following behind him with a book in his hands, like always.

Lucas spits out a million questions to Jack as he tries to answer them all.

"Where did you find her?" Lucas asks hurriedly.

"In the woods, in my cargo net trap."

"Was she unconscious when you found her?"

"Yes," Jack answers.

"Pulse? Breathing?"

"Faint but steady. And yes, she seems to be breathing fine."

Lucas nods and says, "Take her up to my room. I'll grab what I need and meet you up there."

Lucas is a doctor. At least that's what he was in his old life before the apocalypse. Now he's a fucking lifesaver, and we were lucky to find him when we did. He's saved us more times than I can count.

And even though Jack is the more or less leader of our group, Lucas is a close second. They both know how to get shit done. Me, I wasn't a doctor or a Marine in my former life. Nah, I was just a carpenter working for my dad's business that I would own someday. My three favorite hobbies were working, drinking and fucking.

Boy, how things have changed.

I've been putting my carpenter skills to good use out here, though, reinforcing the gates and fences and, thus, keeping us safe. I've also built shit that we needed, and the guys have assured me that I'm worthy of the group more times than I can count.

We all have something to contribute, even Owen, who looks up at me and pushes his black-rimmed glasses farther up his nose with his index finger. He was a scientist with a Ph.D. and probably a few other degrees under his belt; a total brainiac in his old life. And now he helps us run this farm with his crazy inventions that actually work.

Shit, without him, we wouldn't have hot showers. And that is something I could never live without.

Yeah, we're all different, but we all complete this one fucked-up puzzle that would be incomplete without all four of us in it.

Owen and I follow the other two guys with the girl into the house. Jack runs up the steps with the woman, and Lucas goes into the next room to get his medical supplies.

Owen glances at me and asks, "I wonder where she came from?"

"I don't know, but I can't wait to find out," I tell him.

# CHAPTER 4

*Lucas*

THE WOMAN IS dehydrated, malnourished and injured.
But she's alive.

And I plan on keeping her that way.

All four of us haven't left the woman's bedside since she first arrived three days ago. I had to stitch the gash in her forehead with supplies from my medical bag. And we managed to get her awake enough to drink some water, but her eyes were unfocused, so I doubt if she had any idea any of us were even here.

I also cleaned and bandaged some of the cuts and scrapes that littered her hands, wrists, arms and knees.

"So when's Sleeping Beauty gonna wake up?" Jack asks me, folding his huge, muscular arms across his chest.

He's been calling her that since he first brought her to the house. It's a little nickname that's stuck since we have no idea what her real name is. "As soon as she's ready," I tell him with a yawn.

I've gotten barely any sleep over the past few days. And even though I'm dead ass tired, I don't want to leave her side. She's captivated all of us with her beautiful face and peaceful slumber. Even though she's still covered in dirt and has twigs in her hair, she's the most beautiful woman I've ever laid eyes on.

"I'll take the first shift," I call out.

The three guys grumble in response, pissed off that they didn't call dibs first.

"Wake us up if anything changes," Carter mutters, walking out the door with Owen trailing behind him.

"I'll take second shift. I'll be back in a few hours," Jack tells me.

I give him a nod before he goes, half hoping that he'll sleep through his shift, but knowing he won't. That man is like a machine and runs on clockwork. His body seems to know the exact amount of sleep he has, and he can wake up at the same time every day with his internal mental alarm.

I would say it's a Marine thing, but it's more like it's a *Jack* thing.

Yawning again, I sit back in my chair and study the beautiful and mysterious goddess before me. The woman has occupied a lot of my time lately, and I can't say that I mind in the least bit. She's been a much needed distraction for all of us through the mundane pile of shit that is now our lives.

As a doctor, I had grown accustomed to running on hardly any energy and little sleep. My life was busy and good. Fuck, it was good.

The night that everything went to shit will forever be with me as a daily reminder…and a freaking nightmare.

My fiancée, who was also a doctor at the same hospital I worked at, called me on the phone. I could hear the alarms and sirens going off in the background as Sarah was screaming into the receiver at me.

I was woken up out of a dead sleep, exhausted after working a double shift, and I could only comprehend bits and pieces of what she was saying.

*People were dying…coming back to life…killing others…eating people…like zombies…the flu…the vaccine…something was wrong with the new vaccine…so much blood…*

I listened to her die on the phone that night, and there wasn't a damn thing I could do about it. Sarah's screams are forever burned inside my mind, and I'll never forget them.

I lost my fiancée and my entire world as I knew it that night.

And I've never been able to forgive myself for not staying at the hospital. I could have pulled a triple. I could have been there for her, protected her…or at least tried to.

But maybe I would be dead too at this point. So, really, all of this *regret* might just be moot.

I'd stumbled out of my house after the phone call abruptly ended, still in my pajamas, and trying to make sense of everything. But the neighborhood was in pure chaos. People were packing up their shit and hitting the road, leaving everything and even loved ones, in some cases, behind.

The world had become a different place in the matter of just a few days.

I left the house I had a thirty-year mortgage on and traveled north with no destination in mind. When I ran out of gas and couldn't find a station to fill it at, I traveled on foot.

I found a large group of people, and we all headed in the same direction. Our group dwindled down slowly from illness, attacks and other injuries. I ended up being one of the last men standing in a group of four — the same group I'm with now.

We became brothers overnight. Even though we weren't related by blood, we had the same goal in mind — keep each other safe.

We happened upon River's Edge Farm in northern PA by complete accident. But what a happy accident that was. The farm had everything we needed and then some. The prior owners abandoned it. We had no idea why, but could easily figure it out. They were either running too or perhaps looking for their loved ones.

The owners haven't returned since, but we would gladly share the farm with them if they ever did.

We've made a life for ourselves here.

And now we have one more addition to our close-knit group.

I peer down at Sleeping Beauty. Her pupils didn't indicate she had a concussion, so there's really no medical reason causing her unconsciousness. Sometimes the body simply shuts down when the mind is overloaded by too many things. It's as if it's running in protection mode. And I would say she probably needed a lot of protection against the now cruel and vicious world out there.

Even though I've had a couple of years now to grieve the loss of my fiancée, sometimes it feels like eternity wouldn't even be long enough.

And the girl here stirs something inside of me that I thought was gone forever. It's not lust…at least not yet…but a feeling of wanting to protect her from everything bad in the world. It's as if she might be another chance at happiness for me, and I have to grab it and hold onto it for as long as I possibly can.

Gently, I trail my thumb over her jaw and caress her soft cheek. I wonder where she came from and if she has anything or anyone to go back to. The thought of her not being here tomorrow or the next day makes me physically ill. She's become such an integral part of our lives in such a short time that I can't imagine her leaving.

*I hope she stays.*

But what am I even thinking? I mean, seriously…four guys and one girl. It could never work out. *Right?*

Just as I'm contemplating that question, Sleeping Beauty stirs. Her eyebrows furrow as her breathing increases. She's having a nightmare, and I suddenly want to jump in there and save her like her real-life prince.

"Shh," I soothe her, brushing away a stray hair from her face.

She recoils from my touch, and I realize I'm making the nightmare worse. So, I sit back in my chair and watch her carefully.

A whimper escapes her full lips and slowly morphs into an ear-piercing, agonizing scream. Then, she bolts upright in bed, her eyes darting around the room…before they land on me.

# CHAPTER 5

*Trinity*

I AWAKE WITH a start. Someone's screaming, and that can only mean one thing — something found us.

We're not safe.

We're *never* safe.

It takes me a moment to realize the scream is coming from my mouth. The noise dies quickly as I sit up and my eyes shift around the room.

*I must be dreaming.*

I'm in someone's bedroom, and I'm lying on a comfy mattress with sheets and blankets. I haven't had this much comfort in so long that I almost forgot what a blanket against my skin felt like.

I wrap my hands around the soft material, afraid to let go. Afraid to wake up from this wonderful dream.

Movement out of the corner of my eye causes a gasp to catch in my throat as I see a man in a chair beside the bed.

"W-who are you?" I ask. My voice sounds foreign to my own ears. It sounds scratchy and feral.

He holds his hands up in a placating gesture. "My name is Lucas."

He opens his mouth to say more, but suddenly the door bursts open, and a giant of a man comes rushing in.

Terrified, I bolt out of the bed, tripping in the blankets and falling flat on my face before scrambling up and moving to the dark corner of the room. There are a few candles on the other side of the room by the men, and the light illuminates their faces, albeit *handsome* faces.

The one that just came through the door is twice the size of the guy by my bedside. Maybe even *triple* the size. He's huge like some kind of bearded mountain man that could break me in half without breaking a sweat.

I hold my hands out in front of me and yell, "Stay back! Stay away from me!"

The big, bearded guy takes a step back and gives Lucas a sideways glance and a frown. Lucas clears his throat and slowly stands up, but doesn't move an inch towards me. "This is Jack. He's the one who found you in the woods," he explains as if the heroic deed will make me trust the oversized man.

But his tactic does work a little bit, because I'm not so fearful of the giant now. He saved my life, so I owe him the benefit of the doubt at least…and to not try to gouge his eyeballs out if he comes near me.

"What's going on?" I hear another voice ask.

Two more men barrel into the room, their eyes growing wide when they see me huddled in the dark corner like a frightened animal.

"Whoa, she's awake," the one with jet-black hair says. He's shirtless, covered in tattoos with a six pack — no, make that an *eight* pack — with a perfect V visible from his low-riding sweatpants. "Hiya," he says with a big grin. "Name's Carter."

The other one with black-rimmed glasses and sleepy, bedhead hair gives me a shy smile and says, "I'm Owen. Nice to finally meet you." He's also shirtless and putting all sorts of muscles on display.

I glance around at the four of them. They're all so different and all so damn brutally handsome.

*Yep, I'm definitely dreaming.*

I pinch my arm and then hiss in pain when it actually hurts. Okay, so maybe I am awake after all. But how the hell did I even end up here? "W-where am I?" I ask no one in particular.

"You're in our home," Lucas speaks up. "Like I said, Jack here found you in the woods. You were in one of his traps he has set up for large game." He takes a tentative step forward, and I allow it. "You were unconscious, dehydrated and cut up pretty bad."

He motions to my forehead, and my hand instantly goes there, remembering how I hit my head against a rock. Instead of a gash, though, I feel little spiky stitches. *He stitched me up?*

I swallow hard, and it sticks in my dry throat as I try to remember what happened to me after I fell.

*Henry.*

"Who's Henry?" Lucas asks.

My eyes snap up to him. I didn't even realize I had said the name out loud.

"Is he your boyfriend, husband?" Jack demands, his hands curling into fists at his sides. "Why didn't he save you or come back for you?"

I shrink back at the tone of his voice, and Carter puts his hands on the big man's shoulder and says, "Chill the fuck out, dude. You're scaring her."

Jack's frown deepens, and he takes yet another step back, his dark eyes watching me carefully.

"H-Henry was m-my boss at the elementary school I worked at," I explain, keeping my attention on Jack. "Our group…" I swallow back my emotions and wrap my arms defensively around myself. "Our group was slowly dwindling down, and it was just the two of us left." I let out a shaky sigh. "I don't even know if he made it."

Jack studies me for a while before he answers with, "I'll keep an eye out for him when I go back into the woods. If I find him, I'll keep him safe and bring him back with me."

I'm surprised by his kindness, but he *did* find me in the woods and bring me here, after all. Maybe I jumped to conclusions too fast because of his massive size. "Thank you," I whisper to him, and the corner of his lips lift a little. It's not a smile, but it's better than the frown he's been sporting.

Lucas looks back at the others and says, "Let's give her some room and let her rest. We can talk more in the morning."

The guys grumble in response but slowly exit the room.

*He must be the leader*, I conclude.

Lucas stays in the room as the rest leave. His kind, blue eyes make me feel safe, and I slowly begin to unwrap my hands from their protective grip around my middle. My eyes fall on the medical bag on the nightstand and then dart back to him. "Are you a doctor?"

He nods. "Yeah…or I guess I *was*," he says, rubbing the back of his neck with his hand. "You were a teacher?" he asks.

I nod in response. "I taught fourth grade." Tears fill my eyes and my lower lip trembles. "I miss my old life so much sometimes it hurts."

"I know exactly what you mean." He gives me a sad smile. "Hey, look, I'm gonna let you go back to sleep. I'll just be downstairs on the couch."

The thought of him leaving the room scares me. I feel safe with him for reasons I can't even comprehend right now. "Wait," I call out as he moves towards the door. "This is your room?" I ask.

"Yeah."

"Then you should stay here. I can…I can sleep in the chair or on the floor or…"

His eyes widen in surprise when he gets my hidden meaning. "How about you take the bed, and I'll grab a sleeping bag for me?"

I nod in agreement to his suggestion and fight against the smile threatening to surface. I'm glad I didn't have to practically beg him to stay. And I'm certainly glad I don't have to explain why or how he makes me feel so damn safe.

I slowly climb into the bed as he goes to the closet and pulls out a rolled up sleeping bag. He spreads the bag onto the floor beside the bed and lays down, making himself comfortable.

Without even being able to stop myself, I inch over to the edge of the bed and peer down at him. His handsome face and bright blue eyes gaze up at me. And when he flashes me a dazzling smile, I can't even stop the butterflies from erupting in my stomach.

"Thank you for staying," I whisper to him.

"You're welcome," he whispers back. And then his brows furrow as if he's thinking about something important. "Can I ask you your name?"

"It's Trinity."

"Trinity," Lucas says, my name rolling around in his mouth like it belongs there. "We've been calling you Sleeping Beauty. So it's nice to finally have a name to match the pretty face."

My mouth opens in an "O" at his words. And when Lucas realizes what he just said, he tries to backtrack. "I mean, um…uh…"

"It's okay," I tell him with a smile. It's nice to hear someone call me pretty when I've been lost in the woods for months and probably look like grim death. "Goodnight, Lucas," I tell him before lying back on the bed and crawling under the covers.

"Goodnight, Trinity."

With a smile on my face, it doesn't take me long to fall into a deep sleep.

# CHAPTER 6

*Lucas*

I WAKE UP early that morning happy and in a great mood. That's a first...for a long time.

Sleeping Beauty is finally awake, and she has a name — *Trinity*. It's a beautiful name for a beautiful girl.

I roll up my sleeping bag and glance over at Trinity, who is fast asleep. I can already smell breakfast wafting from downstairs, and it smells divine. Carter sure as hell knows how to wake up the people in this house.

We don't have feasts for breakfast very often, only on special occasions, and this is certainly a special occasion.

I watch Trinity as her nose does a little wiggle, and it reminds me of Samantha on *Bewitched*.

She stretches and lets out a low groan that sends a tingling sensation shooting straight to my cock.

*Down boy*, I think to myself. I'm already fighting back morning wood. I don't need to add anything else to the mix right now, or I'll be a walking boner all damn day.

She blinks her stormy, gray eyes open and flashes me a radiant smile that has my breath catching in my throat. "Morning," I manage to tell her with a grin.

"Good morning." She sits up slowly and glances around the room that is now illuminated with natural light. "I don't remember the last time I slept so well," she says with a sad smile.

I nod in understanding. Even though we weren't on the run for as long as she was, I know exactly what she means. It's tough out there in the real world. River's Edge Farm is like a utopia compared to everywhere else.

"I think Carter's got breakfast started. If you want to take a shower and —," I start, but she doesn't let me finish.

"Shower?" she squeaks out in surprise with big, wide eyes.

"Yeah. Thanks to Owen's amazing system he rigged up using solar panels, it supplies power to the pump in the well and the hot water heater in the basement." I can't even try to explain Owen's DIY solar panels and other ingenious inventions. All I know is that it feels damn good to take a hot shower every day. "Just don't stay in too long, and it should stay hot the entire time," I explain to her.

I walk over to the adjoining bathroom and open the door. "Towels are under the sink. And there's some handmade goat milk soap on the tub that you can use."

She stares at me in awe. "Wow, shower, towels *and* soap? You guys are living in a life of luxury. You know that, right?"

I chuckle and nod. "Oh yeah. We know how damn lucky we are." I look at her dirty, threadbare clothes and tell her, "We wash our clothes in the river and hang them up to dry. But I think the previous owners might have something you could wear."

"Wow, thanks. New clothes sound amazing. Wearing the same outfit every day for months gets pretty old," she says quietly.

She stands, and I stare at her loose shirt and sweatpants that have definitely seen better days. "I'll go try to find you some clothes."

She gently rests her hand on my shoulder for a moment as she walks by. "Thank you, Lucas. For everything," she tells me.

I want to tell her she doesn't have to keep thanking me, but I love the sound of her voice and her small touches, so I keep my damn mouth shut.

I watch Trinity disappear into the bathroom and stare at the door for a while. I don't know what the other guys are going to say about her staying here, but there's no way I want to let her go now. I want to keep her. Maybe forever…if she'll let us, that is.

We live by simple rules in this house, and that is to claim what you want. If you want a can of beans or fruit, you claim it, and it's yours. I have about half a mind to claim Trinity, but I don't know how I really feel about that. And I can only imagine how *she* would feel about that…

She'd most likely be turned off by my caveman way of thinking.

First of all, Trinity is so much more important than food or supplies, even though they are vitally important to all of us now. She's a beautiful human being, and it just feels wrong to stake my claim on her.

Nevertheless, I might have to do just that so the other guys stay away. Hell, it's been nearly two years since any of us have even seen a woman. I can only imagine that we're going to be all clambering for her attention…and affection.

Walking down the hall, I go into one of the spare bedrooms of the large farmhouse and sift through the belongings of the former owners. We kind of stuffed everything we didn't need in this room, and I'm glad we kept it all. There are some women's dresses, pants, shoes, the whole nine yards. I grab a big box of stuff and carry it back to my room.

I set the box outside of the bathroom door and holler over the sound of water, "The clothes are out here, Trinity."

"Okay!" she calls back before groaning in pleasure from the first shower she's probably had in a long fucking time.

Her groan goes straight through me again. I picture in my mind the water cascading down over her naked body, and I have to adjust my cock that's suddenly straining against my zipper.

*Fuck, this girl is gonna be the death of me.*

Before going down for breakfast, I quickly change the sheets, thankful that I had an extra clean set in the closet. I ball up the dirty sheets in my arms and head downstairs to talk to the guys.

I have no idea what they're going to say about our new guest. It's not like we've ever had a visitor here before. It's been the four of us for a long time now, and adding someone else to the equation, especially a female, might really throw things out of whack around here.

# CHAPTER 7

*Trinity*

I FEEL LIKE a brand new woman by the time I'm done with my shower. I even used a disposable razor to shave my legs and armpits. I swear my legs looked like I was wearing fuzzy legwarmers twenty-four-seven, and my pits looked like I had Bigfoot in a headlock.

Digging through the pile of clothes in the box, I select a pair of dark gray sweatpants, a burgundy v-neck shirt and sneakers. I even find a pair of panties and socks, which I am grateful for. And even though all the clothes are too big for my thin frame, and the shoes are a little large for my feet, I make them work.

Beggars can't be choosers. Especially not in the world we live in now. I'm just happy to have any clothes at all, especially clean ones.

I comb my fingers through my hair and make myself as presentable as I can, given the circumstances. I have gone without so much for so long that I barely even miss the makeup I used to wear every day or the straightener I used on my hair. Hell, I don't even have a bra on right now. That would have bothered me to no end before…but now I could not care less. I'm just pleased that I was finally able to take a shower. I had been washing with the others in the cold creeks and rivers for so long that I never thought I would experience a hot shower ever again.

Sighing contently, I leave the room. I immediately hear loud, booming male voices downstairs, and I stop short on the landing. I know I should fear being in a house full of men, but for some strange reason, I'm feeling fine.

But all of this is so strange, so surreal. Maybe reality hasn't fully set in yet. I mean, I did fall asleep in a net with a zombie chasing after me and then woke up in an actual bed with sheets and blankets. It's almost like I woke up in an entirely different world.

And besides, there might be other people here too, maybe even other women. Just because I saw four guys in my room last night doesn't mean there aren't other occupants in this large farmhouse.

I make a promise to myself not to totally freak out unless it's completely necessary. Until then, I'm going to play it by ear but also be very cautious.

Tiptoeing down the stairs, not wanting to announce my presence yet, I overhear the conversation coming from the kitchen.

"So her name is Trinity?" someone asks. I think it's Jack, because it's so deep.

"Yes. She didn't tell me much, but I'm sure we'll find out more after she's done with her shower." That's Lucas's gentle voice. I almost have it ingrained in my head.

I reach the last step as the guys continue to talk about me. They have no idea I'm eavesdropping, and I can't help but want to find out what they think about me.

"So which one of us do you think she'll fall for first? If I had to put money on it, I'd say me," Carter says with a dark chuckle. His voice is deep and melodic.

"Fuck you, Carter," Jack pipes up. "Always turning everything into a contest, as usual."

"Speaking of which, I already claimed those canned peaches," he retorts.

Jack simply mumbles in response.

I smile as they bicker back and forth. And then, as I take a step closer, I end up stepping on a creaky floorboard that gives away my presence in an instant.

I cringe and stand stock-still as their conversation ends abruptly. Yep, they definitely heard me.

"Trinity?" Lucas calls.

I walk into the kitchen with what I hope is a friendly smile on my face. The four guys are crowded around a large rectangular wooden table. Their plates are full of food, and there's an empty chair and plate waiting for me.

Lucas pulls out the chair next to him and gestures for me to sit. Once I do, he pushes me in closer to the table. "We weren't sure what you like to eat, but I hope you like eggs."

I look down at my plate full of scrambled eggs, some leafy greens and fresh-picked black raspberries.

*Oh, I could practically weep at the sight.*

My stomach growls and my mouth waters. I haven't eaten a decent meal in what feels like forever. "This is great. Thank you so much," I say vehemently, picking up my fork and forcing myself to eat slowly and to not inhale everything on my plate like some kind of animal. And even though the food is bland since there's no salt and pepper to season anything, it tastes just like heaven to me.

Once I begin to eat, the rest of the guys start digging in too.

"We eat a lot of eggs, but we also fish from the river, and Jack hunts for small game and deer," Carter explains. "It's nice to be able to cook a variety of things instead of having eggs every day."

I can't even imagine getting tired of eating the same thing. I would have killed to have eggs every day when I was out in the woods. My group was living on anything we could get our hands on, which wasn't much. It wasn't abnormal for us to go days without a single ounce of food. It was horrible, and a shiver runs through me at the memories that surface in my mind.

"Are you cold?" Lucas asks from beside me.

*Always the protector.*

I give him a small smile. "No. I was just…thinking of something."

He nods and then takes another bite of his meal.

There's a glass of water beside my plate, and I lift it up and just stare at the clear liquid that's not brown, murky and teeming with bacteria and dirt like I'm used to seeing. I lick my lips before taking a big swig of the cool water, barely holding back a moan as I set the glass back down.

Carter stands up and retrieves a hot mug from the old-fashioned wood stove in the corner of the room. He's wearing a t-shirt today, which I'm thankful for. I don't think I would be able to concentrate with his perfectly chiseled chest on display again.

I gawk at the cup filled with very light green water as he sets it down in front of me.

"It's pine needle tea," Carter speaks up after seeing me eyeing the cup. "It's not coffee; but if you close your eyes really hard, you can pretend it is," he says with a sexy grin.

I take a tentative sip. It's not bitter, but I can taste a hint of pine in it. It's actually really good considering I haven't had anything but river and rain water since the apocalypse. "How did you learn to make this?"

He claps Jack's large shoulder and says, "Jack here is the survivalist amongst us men. He taught me how to forage and make stuff I never even would have dreamed of making before a couple years ago."

I glance at Jack, and he gives me a smirk. He looks even more massive this morning than he did last night in my room. The shirt he's wearing is tight against his muscular chest, and the sleeves are cut off, revealing bulging biceps. He has some tattoos scattered over his skin - an eagle, the American flag with *Semper fidelis* scrawled underneath, and a cross.

He catches me staring and explains by saying, "I was in the Marine Corps."

And with that bit of knowledge, it changes my opinion of Jack completely. He may look like a giant, but he's a protector too, just like Lucas. I flash him a big smile and tell him, "Wow, that's incredible." Then, to keep up the small-talk, I offer, "I was an elementary school teacher."

Carter says, "I was a carpenter. I worked for my dad's company. But I also ran a bar and cooked."

"I was a doctor…but you already knew that," Lucas utters from beside me.

I glance at Owen, who is sitting quietly at the end of the table. He's watching our interactions, but not saying a word. His brown hair is still haphazardly styled on his head, and he studies everyone behind his dark-rimmed glasses.

"What about you Owen?" I prompt.

"Owen is the brains of the operation," Carter says with a grin, answering for him.

"I was a scientist," Owen explains quietly.

"Oh, he's being modest," Carter says with a grunt. "He, like, invented shit and had patents on a lot of his creations."

Owen's definitely the quiet one of the bunch, but I actually find his quirky shyness really sexy. Also, it doesn't hurt that he has a Clark Kent thing going on. He's not as muscular as, say, Carter, but I can definitely see his firm, sinewy forearms as he reaches for his drink.

"So, Trinity, how old are you?" Carter asks.

"I'm twenty-four," I answer.

"A year older than me. I always had a thing for older chicks," Carter says with a wink.

That gets him a punch in the arm from Jack. "Don't mind him. He hasn't seen a female in a very long time."

"None of us have," Carter mutters, rubbing his arm.

My eyes widen at that admission. "So…there are no other people here?"

Lucas shakes his head. "Just the four of us. We haven't seen anyone else in almost two years."

I take a sip of my tea as I process that new piece of information. Okay, so no other females here. I'm feeling suddenly outnumbered and for good reason. *Four against one.* The odds are definitely not in my favor.

But I still don't have a sense of fear from these four men. They have been nothing but kind to me; and until they do something otherwise, I'm going to trust that they will not harm me.

The guys then take turns telling me their ages. It turns out Jack is the oldest at thirty-five with Lucas at a close second at thirty-four, and then Owen four years older than me at twenty-eight.

"Did you guys know each other, you know…before?" I ask quietly.

They all shake their heads simultaneously. "The four of us ended up together somehow when our group started getting picked off one by one," Jack says.

*I know exactly what that's like*, I think to myself.

We finish with breakfast and take our plates to the sink. "I can wash these," I offer to Carter, but he shakes his head.

"Thanks, but no thanks. You're our guest. So why don't you just relax and take it easy for today?"

My stomach drops at his words. Yes, I'm just a guest. And who knows how long they will allow me to stay. They could kick me out tomorrow if they really wanted to. I have no claims to this house or property.

The thought of going back out there on my own terrifies me to no end. I need to prove my worth, that I can be helpful here. But when I ask what I can do to help, the guys all tell me to relax for the day, and my heart sinks.

I retreat to Lucas's room and sit on the edge of the bed, staring out the window. My hands feel around the clean sheets that Lucas must have put on the bed while I was in the shower. The coolness of the material does little to qualm my nerves, however; and pretty soon tears fill my eyes as I try to imagine being out in the woods on my own.

I probably wouldn't last a week.

Maybe not even a whole day.

Curling into a ball on the bed, I allow my emotions to surface, and I eventually cry myself to sleep.

# CHAPTER 8

*Trinity*

THE NEXT MORNING after breakfast, Jack asks me if I'd like to go fishing with him. I practically jump at the opportunity. This will give me time to bond with the giant of a man, but it will also give me a chance to prove my worth to the group.

I've never fished in my life; but I know that if they allow me to stay here, I need to pull my own weight and contribute in some way. I can't expect the guys to dote on me like a princess. And I certainly don't want to spend all day in Lucas's room again doing nothing.

Jack opens the front door and walks outside. I stare at the open door like it's a portal into another world. I haven't been outside in days, and I can feel the fear creeping up my spine already as I step out onto the porch.

After two years of never really being able to put my guard down and always waiting for something to jump out and attack me from around every corner, I can't quite shake the eerie feeling of being in the open with no protection.

The fresh air fills up my lungs as I breathe it in deeply and exhale slowly, taking in the property that's laid out in front of me.

The front porch wraps around the house, and the big yard slopes down a grassy hill to a beautiful, flowing river in the distance. To the right of the property are two large barns and a small shed. To the left is a big garden surrounded by tall wire with various plants growing in the tilled soil.

The old farmhouse itself is massive with two stories, white siding with dark blue shutters.

The guys definitely lucked onto this property. They have a place to grow food to eat, and they must have animals somewhere on the farm considering what we had for breakfast and the fact that they have homemade goat milk soap. Plus, the whole farm looks like it's surrounded by tall fencing and a front gate, keeping unwanted guests out.

On the end of the porch, Jack grabs a small bucket labeled "worms" and two fishing poles before we continue on down to the river.

He walks confidently while I'm the complete opposite. Every step I take I'm afraid of seeing one of *them*. The fence around the property is nice and all, but I'm still afraid that they could get in somehow.

When Jack notices that I'm trailing behind, he stops and says, "You don't have to worry about them, Trinity. The perimeter is secure, and we have precautions in place. We'll hear them before we see them." And then he adds, "Besides, I won't let any harm come to you."

His words make me instantly feel better, but I'm still a little wary. Old habits die hard I suppose.

At the edge of the river that runs through the middle of the property, Jack drops the poles and bait.

"Ever fish before?" he asks me.

I shake my head.

"That's okay. There's a first time for everything, right?" He grabs one of the poles and baits the hook with a long earthworm. "Good thing I'm a great teacher."

He thrusts the rod into my hands, and I stand there like an idiot. I don't even know how to cast the hook into the water.

Jack comes up behind me, and the instant warmth of his massive body feels good against my chilled skin. "Is this okay?" he whispers in my ear.

"Yes," I croak. Then, I clear my throat and answer confidently, "Yes."

He chuckles deeply, and it sends a shiver straight through me. His beard tickles against my neck as he shows me how to grip the rod. He pushes my thumb into a small button and says, "That's to release the line." Then he positions me sideways and shows me how to flick my wrist and launch the hook, bait and sinker into the water. A little red and white bobber pops up, floating above the water. "If you see the bobber go below the water line, that means something's on your hook." Then, he spins the little knob on the side and says, "That will get some tension in your line." He releases his grip on my rod. "And that's all there is to it," he tells me before stepping away. "If you feel something pulling on the line, tug up fast to secure the hook in the fish's mouth."

I instantly miss his warmth. It's a foreign feeling for me to feel safe and protected, and I definitely do in Jack's arms. *Maybe because they are so freaking huge and he could protect a small village inside of them.*

I sneak a peek at him as he readies his rod and casts it out a few feet down river from mine. He's wearing a dark shirt with the sleeves ripped off and ripped up jeans. Most of his face is covered with a beard, but I can tell he's handsome underneath all that scruff. His long, dark hair is tied back with a rubber band, and his dark eyes are studying the water intently.

He doesn't talk much while we fish, but it's nice to have a comfortable silence between us. I'm definitely not used to everything being so calm and peaceful. And it's wonderful.

After a while, I'm the first one to break the silence when I ask him about the animals. "So, you have goat's milk soap and eggs. I take it there are animals somewhere on the farm?" I haven't heard any, and I have no idea how they keep them quiet from the monsters lurking in the woods.

"We soundproofed one of the big barns out back. We have a few goats and several chickens." He draws in his line a little. "They were all here when we got here, so we've been taking care of them."

"And you also trap animals in the woods? Lucas said I was in one of your traps."

"Yep. I trap deer, bear, cougars." He looks over at me and adds, "And pretty girls."

And then, he flashes me a big smile, the first I've ever seen grace his lips. He looks so boyish when he smiles that my heart does a little skip inside my chest. Suddenly, I no longer see him as a large threat. I see him more like a gentle giant.

I turn my attention back to my rod, and that's when I feel a slight pull on my line. "Uh, Jack," I whisper.

He looks over at me and asks, "You got something?"

"I don't know. Maybe." Then, I feel a much sharper tug. "Yeah, I think I do."

He reels in his line and drops his rod before coming over to me. He steps behind me and guides my hands, helping me to reel in the fish that's tugging hard on my line. "Nice and easy," he says, his breath skating across my neck. "That's it."

I settle my back against his hard chest, but I don't think he even notices since he's too focused on the task at hand. His warmth engulfs me, and it feels so damn nice. I watch his biceps bulge as he wraps his hands over mine and tugs on the pole.

"It's a big one," he says, and I have to hold back a giggle because I can't help but think of what else is *big* in this situation.

A long fish jumps up out of the water, and I squeal quietly in delight. I've never caught a fish before, and I suddenly feel extremely proud that I was able to do it.

Jack takes control of the rod and brings the fish out of the water. "Nice catch, Trinity," he says, beaming up at me as he kneels down to take the fish from the hook. "It's a rainbow trout," he tells me as he holds the fish up for me to see the iridescent green and purple colors running along its length.

Normally I would hate to eat something so alive and beautiful, but times are different now. You can't just go to a restaurant and get something to eat. In this world, we have two options: hunt or be hunted.

And I'm going to prove my worth to these four men. I want to prove that I can be helpful.

I just hope that they'll let me stay. At least for a little while.

# CHAPTER 9

*Lucas*

THAT NIGHT WE dine on Jack and Trinity's catch of the day. They managed to wrangle up some beautiful rainbow trout. And I had to laugh when Jack begrudgingly told us that Trinity caught the biggest fish earlier since Jack is so competitive and hates to lose at anything.

As we're gathered around the table for dinner, I can't help but allow my gaze to linger on Trinity for most of the meal.

She's breathtakingly gorgeous and naturally pretty without a stitch of makeup. Her long, auburn hair is secured in a ponytail high on her head with a piece of white ribbon she must have found somewhere. And her stormy, gray eyes make me melt every time she glances my way.

Just having her here is like a breath of fresh air.

And even though the guys and I haven't really discussed anything about her staying long term, I'm pretty sure they're just as enraptured with her as I am.

Carter is pretty much the only one that has voiced his infatuation with her, but he's the most outspoken one of the group. And that's putting it lightly.

"Trinity, would you like me to show you around the farm tomorrow? You can even help me feed the animals," Carter suggests, catching me completely off-guard.

"Sure, that'd be great," Trinity answers him with a smile.

*Damn it*, I mentally curse. I wanted to show her around the farm tomorrow since Jack took up most of her day today. The only real time I get to spend with Trinity is when I'm sleeping on the floor next to her, silently pining over her like a teenage boy.

I could easily go downstairs and sleep on the couch, but there's no way I'm leaving Trinity alone. Just hearing her soft, even breathing at night lulls me into a peaceful sleep like I've never experienced before.

But the past few nights have been torture for me. And it's not because the hard floor is killing my back either. It's because, fuck, I want to do so much more than sleep in the same room as her. I want to touch her, kiss her…make her mine.

If the guys keep stealing her away from me, she might fall for one of them first, leaving me in the dust.

Grumbling, I take my empty plate to the sink, relishing in the fact that at least Carter will be doing the dishes later while I'm alone in my bedroom with Trinity. Even though it's strictly platonic between us for right now, I enjoy spending time with her, nonetheless.

After everyone is done eating, Jack brings out a couple stacks of playing cards. They're battered and torn from use because, fuck, we play a lot of card games. There's not much else to do around here at night. It's not like we can turn on the TV and watch football.

If we end up doing a supply run soon, I'm sure playing cards will be number one on Jack's list of things to keep an eye out for.

It's amazing how much you can miss small things like that until you no longer can just go to a store to buy them. I miss eating Cobb salads and big, juicy steaks. I miss mundane things too like name-brand toothpaste and deodorant. We try to make our own deodorant and soaps and stuff, but it's not the same. Thank god we have a well, hot water and can shower often. Otherwise, we would be stinking up this place to high heaven just from sweating during the summertime.

Jack deals out the cards, and Trinity sits next to me so I can explain to her the rules. Every time I lean in to whisper something to her, I have the urge to pull her in close and kiss those pink, bee-stung lips of hers.

But I keep myself under control and do my best to focus on the card game.

Carter wins almost every hand and gloats to no end. I swear he was a card shark before the apocalypse.

Jack is good at bluffing since he always wears the same serious expression morning, noon and night. That's how he wins most of his hands.

And Owen…he's so damn quiet and shy that no one knows whether he has a good or a bad hand. But he usually ends up folding, so we never really find out either way.

On the last game of the night, it's down to Carter and Trinity. Jack, Owen and I folded early on. Peeking over Trinity's shoulder, I see she has a pretty good hand, but Carter's cocky smirk on his face indicates that his might be a little better.

Carter stares at Trinity over the cards spread out in his hands and asks, "How about we make this more interesting?"

I cock a brow at him. *What game is he playing at now?*

"What did you have in mind?" Trinity asks innocently.

"Winner's choice. So if you win, you can choose something you want…and vice versa."

"And what is that *you* want?" she asks, tilting her head to the side.

He licks his lips, his eyes darting to her mouth before he answers with, "A kiss."

I can see the blush creeping up her cheeks as she tears her gaze away from Carter and studies her cards. *That son of a bitch.* I'm totally convinced he has a better hand now, but Trinity ultimately falls for his charm.

"Fine," she says, glancing at her cards again, outwardly confident in her hand. "If I win, you have to wash everyone's laundry for a week."

Carter chuckles and nods. "You're on."

A smile forms on my lips. Carter hates doing laundry and bitches about it all the time. So, if Trinity can pull this off, she just made his life that much more miserable. Crossing my fingers under the table and hoping that she wins, I watch in anticipation as they lay their cards out on the table.

Trinity has a full house.

And Carter has...a royal *fucking* flush.

"Bastard," I mutter under my breath. He knew the whole time he was gonna win, and he played us all.

"I'll take that kiss now," Carter says with a lopsided grin on his face as he stands.

Trinity swallows hard before standing and going to Carter. All of our eyes are glued on the two of them as she stands before him. I watch as Carter gently cups her cheek in his palm and leans down to press his lips against hers in a sweet, unhurried kiss.

I'm surprised he isn't somehow taking advantage of the situation, but then I watch as he runs his hand along her waist before tightening his arm around her back to suddenly pull her closer and roughly press her up against his chest.

Trinity gasps in surprise at the abrupt movement, and Carter uses that to his full advantage, dipping his tongue into her mouth in a passionate kiss.

Fuck, I want to look away, but I just can't. The way he's kissing her and the way she's going weak in the knees has me riveted. I never considered myself a voyeur, but I begin rethinking that statement when I feel my cock twitch in my pants and lengthen.

Jack, Owen and I sit there helplessly as we watch Carter devour Trinity right before our very eyes. And when he finally pulls back, Trinity has a dazed look on her face like she's never been kissed like that before in her life.

And I'm seeing fucking red.

Standing abruptly and knocking my chair over from the sudden movement, I hiss, "I say we call it a night." Then, I walk out of the room to cool off…and to readjust myself. I'm so damn hard it's almost painful. Watching the two of them together turned me on, but I can't even begin to wrap my head around that.

Trinity rounds the corner and looks up at me with a worried look on her face. "You okay?" she asks tentatively.

My chin jerks as I give her a tight nod before stalking towards the stairs, taking them two at a time up to the landing.

As I stand at the top and listen for Trinity's steps on the staircase, I can hear Jack downstairs double-checking the locks. That's his nightly routine, and it makes me feel safer.

Anything could come in if it wanted in bad enough, but Jack sleeps so lightly that he could probably hear a pin drop from a quarter mile away. He sleeps with a gun under his pillow, and I know he'd take out anyone that would try to harm us.

We have our own alarm systems around the perimeter of the property — old cow bells on trip wires mostly. They're all connected, and if anyone steps on one or gets tripped up on the fishing line, it will let out a resounding chorus of bells, alerting us to approaching danger.

That would be enough to wake us all up, I'm sure. Hell, I don't think Jack is the only one who doesn't sleep soundly. I mean, how can you when the world is like it is today?

I arrange my sleeping bag and pillow on the floor as Trinity goes into the bathroom to get ready for bed, as per our usual routine. She emerges a few minutes later in tiny shorts and a tight t-shirt that must have belonged to a teenager at some point. My eyes peruse her body…the way her long, sculpted legs move towards me, graceful like a dancer…and the fact that the shirt leaves nothing to the imagination, showing off her gorgeous, generous tits…before I snap them shut, effectively blocking her out. And if I thought my cock was hard before…it's made out of pure fucking steel now.

Brushing past her, I mention taking a quick shower, leaving her staring after me in bewilderment at my sudden change of attitude.

Once under the hot spray, I palm my dick and stroke myself. It feels so damn good and takes the edge off immediately, sending a shiver through me. Images of Trinity and Carter making out fill my mind at first, but then slowly I begin thinking of her and me…us kissing…us fucking…

It doesn't take long until I'm so fucking close I can't even think straight. "Oh fuck," I groan, slapping my free hand against the tiled wall as I come, hard, my release washing down the drain.

I stand under the hot spray for a while. I thought getting off would make me feel better, but it doesn't. I'm still pissed off that Carter kissed Trinity in front of all of us. I'm even more pissed off that he probably thinks he *claimed* her now as his.

But I have news for him. I'm not giving her up without a fight.

I slip on a pair of clean shorts and a t-shirt and stare at myself in the mirror as I brush my teeth with the last tube of toothpaste I have in my possession. I scowl at my reflection. I'm mad at myself that I didn't put a stop to the stupid bet. I should have known Carter had an ace up his sleeve, so to speak.

When I walk out of the bathroom, I see that Trinity is lying in my bed, wide awake. We don't say a word to each other as I walk over to the sleeping bag and climb in it. A second later, the room is doused in darkness as Trinity blows out the candles on the nightstand.

I try to fall sleep, but I soon find myself tossing and turning, trying to get comfortable…and trying to get the image of Carter kissing Trinity out of my mind.

"Lucas?" I hear her melodic voice whisper in the dark.

I open my eyes and stare at the ceiling. "Yeah?"

"I know that Carter offered to show me around the farm tomorrow, but…would you want to come too?"

I grin at her words and the hidden meaning behind them. She feels safer with me and wants me with her…even though he kissed her first. "Of course," I tell her, and I can almost sense her smile in the shadows.

"Goodnight, Lucas," she whispers.

"Night."

I know Carter will be pissed, but that makes me smile even wider. I'll be fighting with him for one-on-one time with Trinity, but I know in the end I'll win.

I want her too much to lose.

# CHAPTER 10

*Trinity*

THE NEXT DAY, Carter and Lucas show me around the farm. At first, there's a lot of tension between the two of them; thick enough to cut with a knife. But eventually, they get so wrapped up in showing me around that they forget all about what they're obviously upset about. Not that I actually know what Lucas is upset about, but I'm pretty sure it has to do with Carter kissing me last night.

His entire attitude changed after the kiss, so I can only assume that he's mad or maybe even jealous. The fact that he could be jealous makes me kind of giddy inside, though, because I've been harboring secret feelings for Lucas ever since I first woke up in his bed.

But I'm also torn, because when Carter kissed me, it was like no other kiss I had ever experienced in my entire life. My knees went weak and my head went foggy. His lips and his taste lingered on my mind for a long time last night.

Then there's also Jack and Owen.

While I haven't gotten to know Owen very well yet, he's very attractive and smart and the typical type of guy I would have gone for back in the old world.

Jack, who is the complete opposite of Owen, is also on my radar. When he took me fishing, I definitely found myself becoming instantly attracted to him. He's big and strong and totally the alpha male of the group.

And, *wow*, does that turn me on.

I've never been so insanely attracted to more than one man at the same time, let alone *four*. The whole thing is exhilarating and terrifying all at one.

"Over there is the garden. We grow as many crops as we can to feed ourselves as well as the animals," Lucas explains, showing off his perfect smile and effectively breaking me out of my inner musings.

It's interesting to learn what was here before they arrived and what they've done since then to sustain the land and prolong their stay here. As we're walking to the barns, I notice Owen in the distance hovering over a bunch of what can only be described as car and machine parts laid out on a low table. "What's he doing?" I ask Lucas.

Lucas glances down that way and gets a big grin on his face. "He's working on making a wind turbine with a car alternator so that we can have electric for the house and barns."

"As if his DIY solar panels aren't awesome enough already," Carter pipes up.

"Yeah," Lucas says with a chuckle and a shake of his head. "Thank fuck he came up with that idea. I don't know what I would do without a hot shower every morning."

The guys start walking towards the barns again, but I stand still, staring at Owen from afar. He looks up, notices me staring and gives me a small, awkward wave. I sport a big smile and wave back.

Owen is definitely an enigma wrapped in a riddle. He's so quiet most of the time, but I have a feeling that a million things are swirling around in that big brain of his.

"Trinity, you coming?" Carter calls.

"Yeah," I say, reluctantly turning away from Owen and jogging to catch up with the guys.

Carter unlocks the door and opens it only wide enough for us to go inside. There aren't any lights to turn on, but thankfully the big skylights above provide enough natural light to see. The barn is huge, sectioned off to house different animals.

There are several chickens running around a corral of wire fencing with a chicken coop on the left-hand side. And on the right are five goats playfully head-butting each other.

Lucas walks over to a large bin and lifts the lid. I see that it's filled with numerous labeled containers.

"The chickens eat lots of little critters that we catch outside like crickets and mealworms, plus some crops we grow, even fish. It's tough keeping them fed sometimes, but we make it a priority, because we need the eggs they lay," Lucas clarifies.

"As for the goats, those fuckers will try to eat almost anything," Carter says with a chuckle.

"But we feed them mostly plants and hay," Lucas cuts in.

"We milk them every morning," Carter says, patting one of the goats on the head. "And they also give us some good, stinky fertilizer for our garden."

Lucas reaches into one of the containers and grabs a handful of grain. He throws it over the wire fencing, and the chickens go crazy pecking at the ground to eat it.

"The hens lay eggs almost every day." Lucas opens a piece of the fence and motions for me to go inside. "We usually collect them while they're busy eating. Otherwise, they get pretty protective of their eggs."

Lucas and I collect several eggs, putting them in a small bucket before leaving the same way we came in.

"The goats are more fun to feed," Carter says with a wink. He pushes a handful of hay into my hand and steers me towards the awaiting goats.

They start making all sorts of noise and running towards me as soon as they spot the food. I squeal in fright as they all crowd around me, trying to eat the food in my hand.

Carter and Lucas chuckle in amusement as they watch me try not to get trampled to death.

There are a few older goats, at least one male, two females and two baby goats. The two baby goats eagerly feed from their mothers while they're distracted with the hay in my hand.

It's like being a kid in a petting zoo all over again. They're so damn cute.

Carter brings over more food, and the goats go to him. He kneels down, petting them softly as they eat, and it's nice to see this softer side of Carter.

When he looks up and catches me staring at him, he looks surprised at first. But then he simply gives me his signature smirk and wink.

He's definitely the bad boy of the group, and his body definitely looks like it was made for sinning.

I haven't had sex or even thought about sex for so long. I honestly didn't even know I could still be attracted to another human being. Out there in the wild it's all about fighting to stay alive. No one was focused on relationships or love or much of anything else other than living day to day and staying alive.

I tear my gaze away to find Lucas watching our interaction. Perhaps my lust is written all over my face, but I can't help it.

Being stuck in a house with four attractive men will do that to a girl.

After we're done feeding the animals, we leave the barn and return home.

*Home.*

Even though I've only been here for a short time, it is starting to feel like home to me.

I just hope they let me stay a little while longer.

# CHAPTER 11

*Trinity*

AFTER A FULL day roaming around the farm with Lucas and Carter, feeding the animals, tending the garden and getting a feel for the land, I'm ready for bed right after dinner.

Upstairs, Lucas applies an antibacterial ointment to my stitches so very gently. Thankfully, there are only a few, and he said the scar should be minimal. But let's face it, it's not like I'm going to be competing in any beauty pageants anytime soon.

I study his handsome face up close and personal. His bright blue eyes instantly draw me in. Then, I drift down to his perfect nose and perfect mouth. His face looks like it could have been carved out of stone by a famous Greek artist. He has day-old stubble lining his strong jaw, and I find myself wanting to feel it. Is it soft or prickly? And what would his lips feel like against mine?

"You're all set," he says, breaking me out of my reverie. Then, he stands up to throw away the Q-tip he was using into a small trashcan.

"Thank you, Lucas." It seems like all I do lately is thank him, but he does so much for me. I settle into the bed under the covers and watch as he retrieves the sleeping bag from the corner of the room. For the past week that I've been here, he's slept on the floor. And I feel terrible about it.

The thought of having him sleep next to me in the bed makes me feel two things — safe and scared — at the same time.

In the short time since I've been here, I've grown the closest with Lucas. All of the guys are slowly building up a place inside my heart, but Lucas is the one I've spent the most time with.

While he's spreading the bag on the floor, I suddenly blurt his name out. When he turns to look at me with a raised blond brow, I ask, "Would you like to sleep in bed? With me?"

He swallows hard, his Adam's apple bobbing in his thick throat as he eyes the bed and then turns his attention back to me. "You wouldn't feel…uncomfortable?" he asks gently.

I shake my head. *No. In fact, I think I would feel the exact opposite*, I think to myself.

"O-okay," he says, suddenly seeming shy, and I have to hold back my grin.

Dressed in dark, low-riding sweatpants and a white t-shirt that clings to his muscular chest, he climbs into the bed next to me after blowing out the candles.

The bed is big enough for both of us, but doesn't leave much room in between. We both roll onto our sides and stare at each other in the dark. There's some light from the moon streaming in around the curtains, but it's hard to make out all of his features.

I inch a little closer, my thighs pressed against his. "Lucas," I whisper in the dark.

"Yeah?"

"Will you…hold me?" I ask quietly.

He hesitates for a moment before answering with, "Sure."

I roll onto my other side, and he presses his front against my back, enveloping me in his arms. His fingertips absentmindedly trail up and down my arm, sending a cold shiver tap-dancing down my spine.

"Are you cold?" he asks.

"No." In fact, I feel like I'm burning up. The heat radiating off of him is only fueling the fire stirring deep inside of me. Without even meaning to do it, I wiggle my backside closer to him. But when I do, I can feel the growing bulge of his cock pressing against my ass.

"Trinity," he warns, his voice guttural. "I'm only human. I only have so much restraint," he bites out.

Sinking my teeth into my lower lip, I wiggle again, and this time he wraps his hand around my waist, halting me. I wait for him to make the next move, and it feels like minutes, hours, *years* before I finally feel his lips at my neck. He kisses me softly at first, trailing his lips over my heated skin.

Then, I feel his teeth nipping at my sensitive skin before suckling. *Hard.*

He's marking me. Claiming me as his own. And I welcome it, moaning in pleasure.

His arm at my waist pulls me back against him as he grinds his erection against my ass. "I've wanted you since the moment I first saw you," he confesses against my neck before placing a kiss where his words just touched me.

"I feel the same way," I tell him.

Turning in his arms, I grasp his face in between my palms and pull him in for the kiss I've been waiting so long for. His lips are soft, and the stubble on his jaw is prickly, making the perfect combination and sending me into a tailspin.

He licks at the seam of my lips, begging for an invitation. And when I finally grant him access, he thrusts his tongue into my mouth, devouring me hungrily.

His greedy hands fumble with my shirt, and we break the kiss long enough to slip the material over my head. His hands instantly find my aching breasts, and he kneads them softly while running his calloused thumb over my pebbled nipples.

I groan out loud at the ministration, wanting more of him. So much more.

Lucas pulls away, leaving me aching and needy as he moves off the mattress. I hear the strike of a match, and then there's suddenly light in the room when he lights the candles on the nightstand.

"I want to see you," he tells me, running his tongue over his bottom lip. "All of you." He stands by the edge of the bed and grabs my ankle to pull me towards him. A yelp escapes my mouth at the sudden movement, and he hushes me. "Shh, we don't want anyone barging in on us, do we?"

I shake my head. I couldn't stop this even if the guys did come in. And why does the thought of them watching...or even all of them *participating*...suddenly turn me on a thousand times more?

Pushing that crazy thought out of my head, I focus on Lucas as he tears my shorts off. Falling to his knees, he parts my thighs and places a trail of kisses from my knee up to my inner thigh.

His hot breath skims across my skin, sending a tremor through me in anticipation. And when his tongue glides along my slit, I can barely hold back the gasp and moan of pleasure. He gently pushes a finger inside of me, curving it to stroke against my front wall, and I have to hold back a scream.

I sit up, leaning back on my hands as I watch him devouring me between my legs. And it's the most erotic sight I've ever seen. His eyes meet mine as I cry out his name.

My frantic cries do not stop his torturous ways, however. And pretty soon I'm a trembling mess as he continues to sweep his tongue over my clit again and again.

"I want you to come for me, Trinity," he growls as he adds another finger inside of me, stroking me to oblivion.

And when he begins working his tongue over my center again, I'm unable to hold back any longer, and I suddenly shatter around his mouth.

I fall back on the bed and slap a hand over my lips to stop myself from crying out, but it's so damn hard as I ride wave after wave of pleasure from his talented tongue.

My ragged breaths fill the room, and it takes me a while to come back down to earth.

With a satisfied smirk on his face, Lucas rises and strips off his shirt, revealing a perfect body to match his perfectly handsome face. And when he drops his shorts, I swallow hard at the sight of his impossibly long and thick cock bobbing between his muscular thighs.

He strokes himself as he instructs me to move to the middle of the bed. After I'm where he wants me, Lucas crawls between my legs, planting kisses along the way. My body is vibrating with lust under him, and I can feel my inner core tightening in anticipation.

"Please," I beg him, not wanting to wait another second without him inside of me.

Lucas lines himself up and then enters me, filling me slowly inch by glorious inch. Groaning loudly, he cages me in under him, securing his weight on his bulging biceps. Our faces are close, and I can see the anguish on his face as he takes his time entering me to make sure he's not hurting me.

I didn't know how my first time with Lucas would be, but this is how I imagined it — him making love to me without a sense of urgency or apprehension.

Wrapping my hand around the nape of his neck, I pull his mouth down to mine. We kiss slow. We fuck slow.

But soon it's not enough.

Our kiss gradually becomes heated; lips and teeth clashing. He begins fucking me with deep thrusts, driving me up the wall crazy with desire.

We just can't get close enough or get enough of each other, and I've never experienced that before. It's new and exciting and perfection all at the same time.

*It's us.*

"Fuck, you're perfect, Trinity. You feel so damn good," he pants, his breathing harsh against my neck.

He feels impossibly thick inside me, and I groan as he stretches me, my fingernails digging into his firm ass as he drives his cock in and out of me in a relentless rhythm.

I can feel the pleasure quickly building up inside of me, and it's not long before I reach the precipice and tumble over, my orgasm unfolding in a rush.

"Fuck yes," he hisses in my ear as my inner walls squeeze him tightly.

"Lucas!" I cry out.

He fucks me so deeply that it prolongs my orgasm until I'm nothing but a quivering mess underneath him. "That's it, baby," he whispers. Then, he slams into me one final time before he quickly pulls out, his warm seed spilling out over my stomach and pussy.

Lucas falls to the bed beside me, quickly blowing out the candles before pulling me into his arms as we try to catch our breath. I can hear his racing heart beneath my ear, and it soothes me to no end.

In the quiet and still darkness, Lucas whispers, "That was perfect."

I nod against his muscular chest. "It was." I place a kiss to his heated skin and then snuggle close beside him.

And pretty soon sleep consumes us both.

## CHAPTER 12

*Carter*

LUCAS AND TRINITY are late coming down to breakfast, and the rest of us all have an idea why. Jack, Owen and I already talked, and we all agreed on the same thing — we heard Lucas and Trinity getting it on last night.

And none of us are happy about it.

In fact, I'm downright pissed.

And as the two of them enter the kitchen like a happy fucking couple, holding hands and smiling at each other like the world is nothing but fucking rainbows and puppies, I get even more pissed off. And when I see the small hickey on the side of her neck, it throws me right over the fucking edge.

I kissed her first the other night. And if Lucas didn't get the fucking memo, that means I claimed her first.

Throwing the spatula into the sink, I tell them, "Breakfast was an hour ago. Hope you like cold eggs." And then I stomp out the door like my ass is on fire.

I hear Trinity calling my name as she tears out of the house after me. And then I hear Lucas's voice, and it just adds fuel to the fire.

Once I reach the wooden barn that sits to the west of the house, I rip open the door and head inside. Sunlight shines through the large windows, providing enough natural light to be able to see everything. This building houses mostly farming equipment, and sometimes I like to go here just to think and escape from the world for a bit.

I enjoy tinkering around with the tractors and stuff even though we can't use them because of the noise they would create. But I like to keeping them in working condition just in case this fucking world goes back to normal someday.

I turn just as Trinity marches into the barn closely followed by Lucas.

"Carter, what the fuck is your problem?" Lucas asks, his tone angry and accusatory.

"Excuse the fuck out of me?" I hiss, taking a menacing step towards him. He's definitely pushing all my buttons today. "What the fuck is *my* problem? Oh, I don't know, Lucas. Maybe me and the guys have a problem with you fucking Trinity last night behind our backs!" I yell at him.

The two of them exchange a guilty look.

I release a bitter laugh in response. "Yeah, we all heard you two last night." I shake my head and run my hand over the back of my neck, looking down at the dirty wooden floorboards. "Fuck, the house is so quiet you can hear a pin drop. And it's not like you two were trying to be quiet or anything."

"Actually we were," Lucas speaks up.

I roll my eyes to the heavens. "Whatever, man. It's just..." I allow my voice to trail off. Fuck, I'm not very good at this shit.

"It's just what, Carter?" Trinity asks, walking over to me and placing her small hand on my biceps.

I stare into her stormy, gray eyes and instantly get lost. "I kissed you first. I wanted to be with you first, Trinity. I really like you," I blurt out and then instantly regret it. I sound like a fucking teenager confessing my crush to a girl who sits in front of me in math class.

Trinity's expression doesn't waver, though. Her hand moves up to my face, and she cups my cheek with her palm. Her touch is so soft and so delicate that I cease breathing.

"I like you too, Carter," she whispers.

She glances back at Lucas, who gives her an almost imperceptible nod. And then, Trinity turns her attention back to me, hooking her hand around my neck and bringing my mouth down to meet hers.

The kiss is fucking magical and just like how it was the other night between us. Her bee-stung lips are soft, and they mold to mine perfectly. My tongue strokes between them and tangles with hers in a heated kiss.

My greedy hands wander over her body, crushing her tight, lithe form closer to me. She's perfect in every way, and it's been way too long for me to be gentle. Hell, when I kissed her that night, I wanted to drag her back to my room like a fucking caveman. And if she keeps kissing me like she is, I may just do that.

We kiss until we're both needy and breathless. And when we part, I see Lucas staring at us with an indecipherable look on his face. He doesn't look upset or mad. No. If anything, he looks…turned on. Just like the other night.

All the jealousy and anger from this morning fuel my next move as I abruptly lift Trinity in my arms and place her down on a workbench. She lets out a small squeak in surprise, but doesn't protest. Instead, she looks up at me with curiosity and lust in her eyes.

Ever since I first laid eyes on her, I've dreamed about doing this. I'm still pissed that Lucas got to experience it with her first and one on one, but at this point I'll take whatever I can get just so I can have her.

I've never been the jealous type, but Trinity gets my blood boiling.

Going to my knees before her, I take my time unbuttoning and unzipping her shorts before sliding them down her beautiful, long legs. She doesn't have any panties on underneath, and it drives me fucking wild.

She's completely bare down there, freshly shaved, and her lips are glistening already with the evidence of her arousal.

Grabbing her legs, I push them apart and place a kiss on her inner thigh. She leans up, gazing at me as I inhale her clean scent. I can't help but wonder if they showered together this morning...if they fucked in the shower...

Growling in frustration at my jealousy, I hook my hands under Trinity's ass and roughly pull her towards my mouth. I take no mercy on her as I devour her, relishing in the sounds of her sudden whimpers and cries.

I lick, suck and bite gently, feasting on her like a desperate, starving man. And I feel like I've been starving for her ever since she first arrived.

I lick the soft lips of her sex as she squirms under me. Wrapping my arms around her thighs, I hold her in place as I focus my efforts on her clit. I want to make her feel everything I give her without being able to move away, and it drives her crazy with lust. She shakes her head back and forth in silent protest, but it's too late to back out of this now. I'm too far gone.

My cock presses painfully against the zipper of my pants as I feast on Trinity. I slip a thick finger inside of her and groan. So damn warm and tight. Fuck, I can't wait to feel her wrapped around my cock.

I lick and nibble her clit before diving back in to claim her. Hard.

Out of the corner of my eye, I see Lucas round the bench. When he gets near Trinity, she reaches for him. If she wants him to join in, I'm sure as hell not gonna stop her. I've participated in threesomes before, and they can be fun and hot as fuck.

Lucas unbuttons Trinity's flannel shirt, revealing her perfect, beautiful tits. Her little, rosy nipples are hard, and I watch as he runs his thumbs over them. She presses her tits further into his hands in response, and Lucas massages them, plucking at her nipples.

As Lucas leans down to place his mouth over hers, I bury two thick fingers deep inside her. He swallows down her muffled cries as I curl my fingers and stroke her inner walls while working her little, sensitive nub with my tongue.

As I finger fuck her, her juices slide down my hand as the wet walls of her pussy tighten around me, making me groan out loud at the sensation.

I fucking need to be inside of her. It's a need I've never felt before, like I might explode if I don't feel her wrapped around my hard cock soon.

My mouth closes over the little nub of nerve endings, and Trinity shatters around my mouth, gasping my name. And, fuck, my name sounds so hot coming from her sexy, little mouth. It makes my dick hard as stone.

She goes limp under Lucas's hands on the bench as I stand up, unbuttoning and unzipping my pants to free my cock. My hand grips my hard length, and I slowly drag the tip along her wet, swollen seam, teasing her.

She moans at the sensation, and it's music to my ears.

"You want this?" I ask her, and wait for her to nod yes. Then I tell her, "I want you to suck Lucas off while I fuck your tight, little pussy."

Her lust-filled gaze meets mine and then trails up to Lucas, who runs his fingers through her hair and nods reassuringly. Without a word, she begins to unzip Lucas's pants. When his erection bobs free, Trinity's pink tongue darts out and licks around his crown.

And, fuck, it's hot.

When his cock disappears between her bee-stung lips, I'm a fucking goner. Not wanting to wait another second without being inside of her, I bury my dick balls deep into her tight, wet channel.

Trinity cries out around Lucas's cock, and it spurs me on to take her harder and faster. I piston my hips, my cock gliding easily against her slick walls. She's so damn wet for me. I hiss out through clenched teeth. Fuck, she feels amazing.

I can't take my eyes off the two of them. How she looks lovingly up at him, and how he gazes down at her like she's his whole world as he slowly fucks her wet mouth. Fuck, they have an unbreakable connection. And I suddenly want that with Trinity too.

I want her to look at me as if I could save her from the world burning down around us.

Grasping her hips in a bruising grip, I pump in and out of her.

Taking her raw like this only makes my cock grow harder and longer inside of her. I've never had sex without a condom before, but it's not like we really have much of a choice now. And I know we're all clean; we've told each other as much in the past.

Lucas's hips pump upward into Trinity's working mouth. I can tell he's close by the way his jaw is clenched tight and ticking with restraint. "Fuck, Trinity," he growls. And then his thrusts grow erratic as he erupts inside of her mouth and onto her lips.

Her tongue darts out to lick up his seed, and it sends me over the fucking edge. I fuck her until I feel hot sparks shooting down my spine and straight into my balls. Pulling out, I jack off all over her flat stomach, marking her with my come.

Lucas stares at my seed covering Trinity, and I can tell he's pissed off about it. He's jealous just like I was. Well, now we've both fucked her, so he can just get over that possessiveness. Obviously she wants both of us.

And maybe even at the same time again.

Grabbing a clean rag, I gently wipe Trinity clean. Lucas helps her stand, and we both zip up as we watch her get dressed.

Her body is thin from having survived out there for so long in the wilderness, but I can imagine her curves really starting to fill out once we start getting some real food into her. And then I start to imagine something totally out of the ordinary for me.

I imagine her belly swollen with my child.

Shaking the thought from my head, I stare at her and blink a few times to clear the image from my mind.

I don't know what spurred that crazy thought, but it is just that — *crazy*. Trinity might bail on us next week and leave. Who knows what the future holds.

But suddenly, I want her to be in mine. Forever.

# CHAPTER 13

*Trinity*

AFTER OUR LITTLE tryst in the barn, Lucas and I go inside to eat our breakfast that we didn't get a chance to eat earlier.

We eat in uncomfortable silence. And as time goes on and he doesn't speak a word or even glance my way, I'm practically on the verge of tears.

I'm in my head thinking that I lost Lucas from what I instigated. I don't even know who I am anymore. In my old life, I never would have had a threesome. Yes, the thought had crossed my mind a few times while I was enjoying time with my battery-operated boyfriend, but I never thought it would actually happen.

And now that it has, I'm afraid that Lucas has regrets. That has to be the reason behind his silence. What if he throws me out on my ass because of what I did, which feels mostly like betrayal at this point?

Tears begin to trickle down my cheeks, so I quickly get up and take my plate to the sink. I feel Lucas's warm presence behind me, and he suddenly turns me in his arms and pulls me close to him, pressing his lips to mine in an intense kiss.

When he pulls back, I can see the trepidation in his eyes. "Are you okay with what happened earlier?" he asks, his voice barely above a whisper.

"Are you?" I throw the question back to him.

His blond brows furrow. "Yes," he says cautiously. "I didn't think I would be, but fuck, I can't stop thinking about it."

And then he presses up against me, showing me the evidence of his arousal. I gasp at the sensation. Okay, so he wasn't sitting there brooding and being angry at me. He was sitting there thinking about what the three of us did earlier and getting turned on.

"I'm jealous as fuck, though," he says, running his hands through my ponytail and gripping hard. "I don't mind…*sharing* you…but I want you to be mine," he says, his voice deep and gruff. Holding me in place, his mouth claims mine, taking me exactly how he wants.

Inside, I'm thrilled that he's not mad. He's just insanely jealous. I did choose to sleep with Lucas first, after all. He clearly staked his claim on me, and I have no problem with that. I feel closest with him out of all four guys.

There's just the small problem of me being attracted to…*all* of them.

But right now it's just the two of us, and in this moment I want to give him what he needs to hear, some reassurance. Pulling back to stare into his gorgeous blue eyes, I tell him breathlessly, "I'm yours."

Growling in response, he reaches down to undo my shorts and pull them down my legs. Even though I'm a little sore from earlier, I can't help but want Lucas inside of me right now.

He pulls his pants down to his thighs, wraps my legs around his waist and enters me in one, long stroke. I cry out his name, locking my arms around his neck as he thrusts inside of me in a torturous rhythm.

Lucas's fingers dig into my backside as he drives me down on his hard length. "Fuck, you feel so damn good," he breathes into my neck.

There's nothing nice and sweet about this like the first time when we made love. No, this is feral, primal fucking in the middle of the kitchen where any of the guys could walk in on us.

"Tell me you're mine," he demands against my skin.

"I'm yours. All yours," I whisper in his ear.

My eyes drift open, and I notice a figure in the doorway leading to the living room. Owen is standing there, slack jawed and watching us. His hazel eyes pierce mine behind his glasses as he stares at me.

Owen doesn't announce his presence or even make a move from the spot he's standing in, and I can't help but wonder how long he's been there.

Lucas's back is towards him, so he has no idea Owen is even watching. But I do. And it turns me on, fueling the fire that's building up inside of me until I detonate around Lucas's hard cock inside of me.

I cry out in ecstasy, and my eyes squeeze shut as the orgasm washes over me with violent crescendos. Lucas drives his hips up towards me, milking every ounce of pleasure he can get out of me until he joins me in bliss.

He quickly pulls out, spilling his warm release between us.

Lucas presses me up against the countertop and cupboards, panting. "Fuck, Trinity. That was so fucking hot." He kisses along my neck, and I wrap my arms around him, holding him close to me.

And when I peer over his shoulder, Owen is gone.

## CHAPTER 14

*Lucas*

BY THE TIME Trinity and I shower and get dressed for the *second* time this morning to meet Carter outside in the garden, he has that pissed off look on his face again. He's impatient, to say the least, and we definitely took our time eating breakfast…and fucking. Not that he knows what happened after we were done eating.

But when he looks us up and down and realizes we changed clothes, I can pretty much read the look on his face that he knows something happened between Trinity and me.

"Took you long enough," he says, throwing the offhanded comment over his shoulder as he walks to the shed to grab some tools.

Trinity is quiet, but I can see the guilty look on her face. She looks up at me, and I grin down at her. Capturing her hand in mine, I give it a quick kiss before releasing her.

In the short time that I've known her, I've grown very fond of Trinity. I don't know if I'm talking the big L word yet, but fuck, I could see myself with this girl forever without even trying.

When she told me she was mine, I almost exploded with pride and joy. Being stuck on this farm with three other guys is gonna be tough. I mean, they have needs too. And if she wants to sleep with them, I won't stop her. But I want her to always come back to me, sleep in my bed every night, be mine in every sense of the term.

I'll protect her, take care of her, always be there for her. And I want her to know that. As soon as the time is right, I'll tell her. Everything.

"Hey, Lover Boy," Carter calls to me. He barely gives me a heads-up before throwing a hoe at my head. I, luckily, catch it before it hits me in the face. "We have some actual work to do, if you're done daydreaming."

He's still acting kind of pissed off, but he's giving me a playful smirk that tells me he's okay with whatever happened between Trinity and me after breakfast. He hasn't laid claim to her like I have, and I'm glad. Because I sure as heck would put up one hell of a fight.

Over the next few hours, the three of us tend to the garden. We show Trinity how to plant and how to harvest. Carter knows a lot more about gardening than I do because he spent a lot of time at his grandfather's farm growing up. So, I take his direction and advice when it comes to stuff like this.

We also show her the root cellar where we store a lot of our vegetables and some of the homemade canned goods that were from the previous owners. The cellar really comes in handy over winter, supplying us with lots of things to eat even when food was scarce everywhere else and we couldn't utilize the garden.

Trinity is in awe of everything we have on the farm. And even though we weren't out in the fucked-up world for as long as she was, I can imagine how things are getting out there.

I'll always thank my lucky stars we ended up on this farm that provides us everything we need to survive and then some. I don't know how long we'll be able to keep it like this. Eventually, people might come to try to take it from us, but we're prepared to do whatever we need to do to protect what we now consider our home.

And now that Trinity is a part of my life, I'm prepared to protect her too.

She emerges from the root cellar, and there is a smudge of dirt on her cheek. I pull her close and wipe off the smudge with the corner of my shirt. And then I can't help but kiss her full lips. Her arms wrap around me, and the kiss soon turns frenzied.

But the sound of someone clearing their throat has us breaking apart. Carter is standing there, leaned up on the side of the shed with a smirk on his face. "If you two are done making out, we have some veggies to gather for dinner."

We walk past him, and he gives me a clap on my shoulder and a nod of understanding.

We have a simple system on the farm. If you want something, you claim it as your own, and nobody else messes with it unless you offer it.

I think Carter understands that Trinity is mine and I'm claiming her as such with my actions.

But I also think he's wondering when and if I'm going to share her again.

The fucked up part is...I'm wondering the same exact thing.

## CHAPTER 15

*Trinity*

OWEN IS EXTREMELY quiet during dinner. And I mean even more quiet than usual. He keeps stealing glances between Lucas and me. But every time he meets my gaze, he looks away with an indecipherable expression on his face.

I don't want to call him out in front of everyone, so I make a mental note to catch up with him soon to talk things over. I want to find out what's going on in that brilliant mind of his. Maybe he doesn't even want me here, but I'd rather know that now than find out in the future.

I wonder if it would be majority rules in a situation like this. If they all agree I can stay, then I stay. But if not…what would my fate be?

I haven't even discussed my possible future here with Lucas. I'm too afraid to even think about the possibility of going out there on my own. It's been like a dream staying here, and I'm not ready to burst that magic bubble just yet.

Jack clears his throat and looks at me pointedly. "Trinity, would you like to go for a walk in the woods with me tomorrow? I need to check the traps and could use the help…and the company."

I perk up at the opportunity. I still need to prove my worth here, and what better way than helping Jack with catching food that we all eat?

"Sure, Jack, I'd love to."

And then he does something that is very rare for Jack. He actually smiles. It lights up his whole face and changes his entire appearance. He's mostly quiet with a stern look all the time, but I know it's because of what he's been through in his life. Lucas told me a little bit about Jack's background and how he served in the Marine Corps and saw horrific things while doing tours in Iraq.

Things like that can change a person. But I know deep down Jack is a great guy, and I'm excited to spend some one-on-one time with him.

"Try to find a pair of boots if you can," he suggests.

I give him a nod in agreement. Yeah, I'm definitely going to have to rummage through the stash of clothing in the spare bedroom upstairs. I definitely don't want to go into the woods wearing shorts and sandals, which has been my normal attire over the past few days.

After dinner, I go upstairs to find clothes to wear while the guys stay downstairs playing poker.

I manage to find a pair of boots that are a little big, but they'll do just fine. I grab a pair of jeans and a long-sleeve shirt and place them all in Lucas's room for me to change into tomorrow.

When I venture downstairs, Carter, Jack and Lucas are gathered around the table. "Where's Owen?" I ask.

Carter shrugs. "Probably in the library, reading."

"There's a library?" I wonder out loud.

"Well, Owen turned what once was a family room into a library. He's been working on gathering books during every supply run we go on."

So the guys go on supply runs. That sounds dangerous, but I'm sure there are things they've needed that weren't here.

"Which way is the library?" I ask Carter.

He hooks his thumb towards the other room. "Just go through there, and keep going around until you hit it."

As I walk, I realize I haven't explored the house much. I've been too busy exploring the outside property and buildings.

The house is dark, and I move carefully through it, wishing I would have asked for a candle or something.

But I see light at the end of the hall, and I make that my destination.

When I enter the room, I see Owen running his fingers over the spines of books on a large shelf. The room is illuminated by several jar candles spread throughout the space.

"Owen," I whisper, startling him.

He turns around to see me in the doorway, and he instantly relaxes. "Hey, Trinity." He stands and pushes his glasses up his nose, a move I find cute and sorta sexy.

Owen's wearing a button-up blue and white striped shirt with the sleeves rolled up his muscular forearms. He's not the brawniest of the group, but I've seen his lean muscles a time or two to know he's buff.

I want to ask him about earlier today, but I don't want to just blurt it out first thing. Instead, I ask him, "What are you doing?"

He turns towards the shelf, and then I notice the piece of paper and pen laying there. "I'm writing down which books I have and which books I'd like to find." He shakes his head and gives me a sexy grin. "I know it sounds stupid, but finding books has almost become like a treasure hunt. Something to look forward to, I suppose."

"That's not stupid at all," I tell him vehemently. "I love books too, so I know how important they can be to someone." Books have always been like an escape to me, especially when I was growing up in the foster system, bouncing from family to family, house to house. Books were always my constant. My *only* constant.

My words seem to appease him, because his shoulders visibly relax. "If you have any requests, I could try to find it on our next supply run."

*Hmm, so he's planning on me staying for a little while at least*, I think to myself. That makes me smile that Owen doesn't want me to leave and instead wants me to help build his library. "I love Emily Bronte," I offer.

His eyes light up, and he goes to a different bookshelf where several Bronte novels are located. "*Wuthering Heights* was one of the first books I was able to add to my collection."

*Wuthering Heights* is one of my all-time favorite books, so I'm happy to learn that I can reread a great classic while trying to forget about the world for a while. "What about Jane Austen?" I inquire.

"*Pride and Prejudice* is here and so is *Emma*," he says, pointing. "I don't have very many of hers, but I can add them to the list, if you want."

"*Sense and Sensibility?*" I request.

I watch as he moves back to the other shelf to scrawl the book name down on the piece of paper. His tongue sticks out of the corner of his mouth while he writes, and it makes me smile. I find all of his little idiosyncrasies endearing.

"If you can think of any others you'd like, let me know," he says as he finishes writing.

I stand there for a moment, not sure if I want to bring it up, but knowing that I ultimately have to clear the air. "Owen, about earlier today…in the kitchen…" I say quietly, my voice trailing off at the end.

He sets the pen down and squeezes his eyes shut. "Listen, Trinity… I didn't mean to…I mean…" He stops talking and turns to me with his eyes still closed. "You must think I'm a total creep."

I grab his hand and hold it between mine. His skin is soft and warm to the touch. "No, Owen, I don't think that at all. I just…I don't know what to think." He's always so quiet and shy around me, never opening up, never talking more than necessary. "Sometimes I think that maybe you don't even like me or want me around," I confess.

His eyes snap open upon my admission, and he gets a serious look on his face. "I like you Trinity. I *really* like you." It's nice to hear the words coming from his mouth. "I'm just…I'm not very good around women. Never have been. I'm so awkward and a total geek. Always saying the wrong things at the wrong times…like right now," he says, shaking his head slowly.

"Owen, you're not a total geek," I tell him with a chuckle. "And if you are, then you're the hottest geek I've ever seen in my life."

He gives me a bitter laugh. "I didn't always look like this, you know," he says, sweeping his hand downward. "I was just a skinny, pasty white guy stuck in a lab, working too many hours to ever go out on a date."

I try to picture him as skinny and pasty when all I see now is a buff, tanned guy who gives me butterflies when his hazel eyes lock on mine. *The apocalypse definitely did his body good.*

"I never even had a girlfriend," he admits.

Never had a girlfriend? So he's never... Before I can even dwell on the fact that Owen might be a virgin, I hear Lucas calling my name. They're probably all going to bed. I've lost track of time since being in this room.

"Coming!" I call out the door before turning back to Owen. "I want to talk to you again about this...about everything." Owen is so fascinating that I know I need to spend more time with him to crack open his enigmatic exterior.

"I'd like that," he says with a small smile.

I let go of his hand and lean up on my tiptoes to plant a kiss on his cheek. "Goodnight, Owen."

I turn to leave, but he suddenly grabs my hand and halts me in my tracks. "Trinity, wait." I watch as he walks over to the bookcase and grabs the copy of *Wuthering Heights*. He places the book in my hands, and I cradle it against my chest.

"Thanks, Owen," I tell him with a smile before walking out of the room.

Owen may think he's awkward and geeky, but what he doesn't know is that he's slowly stealing a piece of my heart.

# CHAPTER 16

*Trinity*

IT FEELS STRANGE to be back in the woods again, but I feel safe with Jack by my side. He may seem more like machine than man sometimes, but I know deep down he's a big, giant teddy bear with a good heart.

Our time alone allows him to share with me about the time he spent in the Marine Corps, how many lives he saved, and just how hard it was to survive on a daily basis. He's a hero in every sense of the word, but he's so humble about it that it makes me admire him even more.

"It was hard to return back to civilization," he confesses to me. "A car backfiring would set me off like no other. It took me a while to... adapt. And I don't know if I ever fully did."

His large palm is on the small of my back, leading me into the woods. "And now the world sort of adapted to you," I suggest.

He stops walking, and I stop too. He looks down at me with raised brows. "You know, you're right. I never really thought of it like that. But the world as it is today...it reminds me of my time over in Iraq. Always on my toes, looking for the next threat, and protecting my fellow soldiers with my life." A deep, bitter laugh escapes him. "Maybe that's why I feel so much more like myself nowadays. I'm in my element again I suppose." Then, his dark brows lower as he grows very serious once again. "Do you think it's wrong to feel like that?"

"Not at all," I tell him, putting my hand on his muscular biceps. "I think you're one of the bravest and kindest men I have ever met."

Sliding his hand into my hair, he tugs to the point of pain as he leans down and drags my mouth to meet his in an all-consuming kiss. The woods around us disappear as he takes me just how he wants, keeping his rough grip in my hair, as he kisses me into obscurity.

When he finally releases me, my knees are so weak that I actually wobble. "Wow," I gasp, not fully grasping what just happened between us. I knew the chemistry was always there; I just didn't know it would feel like...*that*.

"Fuck, I've been wanting to do that," he breathes against my lips. A squirrel scampering up a tree next to us has his connection to me snapping. He blinks and refocuses his gaze on the forest. "Let's go to the first trap and see if we caught anything."

Jack kneels by a small trap that he calls a *simple spring pole snare* and teaches me how to set it. It takes a lot of practice to learn how to set up the sticks just so, so that the trap will capture whatever sets off the trigger, but I'm slowly learning. Jack is a great teacher, just like he told me the first day we went fishing.

When I finally get it, he smiles and says, "That's my girl."

My teeth sink into my lower lip at his words, and I have to keep myself from breaking out into the biggest grin ever. Jack is very possessive when it comes to certain things in his life, and I love when he exerts his dominance over me.

We move to another trap; and Jack holds my hand, guiding me to make sure I don't trip or fall.

We're about twenty yards into the woods when Jack stops suddenly. When I glance up at his tight face, I know he's on high alert; and that scares me.

"Don't move," he whispers to me.

I'm not planning on moving. Hell, I'm barely even breathing at this point. I'm too frightened.

"There!" he hisses, pointing up ahead of us.

And there, in the thick brush by a small creek, I see a large buck. I let out a sigh of relief since I thought Jack had thought he heard something else, one of *them*.

I haven't seen a zombie since that fateful day when I ended up on the farm, and I don't want to see one ever again.

Jack readies his gun and aims it at the magnificent creature. I look away, not wanting to see him kill the animal. I know we need the food, though, so I can't condemn him for killing the beautiful beast.

A shot rings out, and I look up to see the deer running in the opposite direction. Jack missed? He never misses. He told me so himself. He was the best sniper on his team.

Before I can even comprehend what's happening, Jack calmly tells me, "Trinity, run back to the house."

And that's when I see the group of creatures emerging from where the deer just ran from. There are at least three of them, maybe more. Jack must have taken one out, and now they're all coming towards us from hearing the gunshot.

"Go, Trinity! Now!" he demands.

I take off running towards the edge of the woods that meets the clearing just like that day when I got caught up in Jack's trap. I don't want to leave Jack behind, however, so I keep glancing back to make sure he's okay.

I hear three more shots ring out, and each one makes me jump. With tears building in my eyes, my vision is blurry, and I barely see what's in front of me before it's almost too late.

Skidding to a stop, I see a small group of zombies stumbling towards me from the clearing. They must have heard the gunshots.

"Jack!" I cry, turning and running back towards him.

"Trinity!" he roars.

Oh god, if anything happens to him, I don't know what I'll do. I run as fast as I can with the zombies close behind. I stumble, fall, pick myself back up again and run again.

"Trinity!" Jack calls.

He comes to my rescue, dispatching all three zombies with a large hunting knife, sticking the blade right into their brains. They fall into a messy heap at his feet.

I'm a sobbing mess by the time he's done. And then, he picks me up in his strong arms and carries me to the edge of the woods, setting me down beside a large oak tree.

His hands roam over my body, looking for cuts, scrapes, *bites*.

"Are you okay?" he asks, his dark brown eyes searching my face.

"I am now," I cry.

He kisses my cheeks, tasting my tears. "Fuck, I thought something happened. I thought I lost you," he whispers in anguish, kissing every inch of my face. "I don't know what I'd do without you."

Jack is the strong, silent type. So, for him to be voicing his true feelings for me is something new and wonderful.

"Oh, Jack," I gasp. My palms grasp his face, my fingertips digging into his beard and strong jaw as I pull his mouth to mine. His lips are soft in comparison to the rough beard scraping against my face, and I can't get enough of the combination of sensations.

Jack's hand moves to my nape, pulling me impossibly closer as he consumes me, owning me completely. His tongue battles with mine, but he wins, of course, taking total control.

His other hand skims down my body, slipping underneath my jeans and stopping at the apex between my thighs. His fingers swipe along my already wet slit, and he groans into my mouth.

His thumb presses against my clit as he pumps a finger in and out of me, and he swallows down my cries as I writhe under him. Everything he does feels like heaven, and I can't get enough.

"Please, Jack," I beg him. "I want you inside of me."

He pulls back with a growl and stares at me with a feral look on his face. "Fuck, Trinity. I want that too," he whispers.

Leaning down, he yanks my jeans, along with my panties, down my legs. My boots, which are too big for me, easily go with them as he throws everything down on the ground beside us.

Next, he unbuttons his jeans and pulls them down over his hips, letting his long erection bob up to his stomach.

My eyes widen at the sight. Oh my god, he's huge. Just like I imagined he would be.

He smirks at my reaction and fists his large cock in his hand, pumping once, twice, three times as my mouth practically waters at the sight.

Hooking my right leg under his arm, he positions himself between my legs, moving the head of his cock back and forth along my slit until he's completely covered in my arousal.

"Try to stay quiet," he warns as he lines his thick length up with my entrance and impales me in one, swift stroke.

My teeth sink into his muscular shoulder, clamping down through his shirt as I try to muffle my scream.

"Fuck, this is exactly how I imagined you would feel wrapped around my cock," he whispers against my neck, his breath tickling my skin. "I'm gonna move now, Trinity. We don't have much time out here."

I nod in agreement against his chest. But I don't think I realized just what I was agreeing to. Because as he starts to move inside, I feel like I'm going to split in two.

"Oh, shit!" I hiss against him as he ravages me with his cock.

His adept fingertips move to my clit and rub while he fucks me unhurriedly, rocking in and out of me. After a few minutes, the pain begins to subside, and it feels like pure ecstasy with my walls clamping down on his driving length.

With a growl, he picks up my other leg so that both of them are cradled in his arms as he fucks me raw against the tree, the bark digging into my back. It's dirty and raw and exciting and crazy…and all of those things combined, but I wouldn't trade this moment for anything else in the world right now.

Jack leans in, devouring my mouth, hungrily, without mercy and swallowing my moans and cries that I can't seem to contain. His arms vibrate with strength and power as he takes me.

Unable to hold back anymore, he sends me straight over the edge, and I whimper against his mouth as the orgasm detonates within me, completely destroying me.

Jack pulls back and stares into my eyes as he grits his teeth. "Fuck, you feel so good, Trinity," he growls in a heady whisper that's deep and primal. Gently, he lowers my legs so that my feet are once again planted on the ground.

Then, he spins me around and enters me from behind. I thrust back against him, taking it all and wanting everything he wants to give. I can feel another orgasm building up inside of me, and I have to sink my teeth into my arm to keep from screaming out as pleasure rips through me.

"That's it. That's my girl," he barks possessively.

His thrusts become erratic the closer he gets. And then finally, he pulls out of me and lets out a feral roar that makes me shiver as his come shoots out in stripes against my backside.

"Fuck," he hisses, leaning over me to catch his breath. His mouth finds my neck, and he suckles gently at my skin, wrapping his one arm around my waist to hold me close.

After we calm our rapidly beating hearts, Jack steps back. "Don't move," he tells me.

I look over my shoulder at him in awe as I watch him rub his release into my skin, effectively marking me. Damn, he *is* possessive.

He slaps my ass for good measure when he's done and gives me a panty-melting smirk. "Mine," he whispers.

I can't help the giddy feeling building up inside of me as we get dressed and walk back to the house. My legs feel like Jell-O, and Jack holds my hand the entire way.

When we reach the house, Carter, Owen and Lucas are all standing there with worried looks on their faces.

"We heard the gunshots," Lucas says.

"Everything okay?" Owen asks.

Jack gives them a nod. "Oh yeah. More than okay. Just seen a few creatures, but I took them all out."

Lucas and Owen look relieved, but Carter has a mischievous grin on his face. "And then you took something else, didn't you?"

Jack smiles an actual smile as he looks down at me and says, "Yeah. And it was good. So fucking good."

## CHAPTER 17

*Lucas*

WHEN JACK AND Trinity come back from their hunting trip, I instantly notice a change between the two of them. Jack is looking at Trinity like she's good enough to eat, and she's gazing up at him like he's her protector from everything bad in the world.

I've seen that look in her eyes before. She used to look at me like that.

*Fuck.*

"Yeah, and it was good. So fucking good," Jack says, breaking through my thoughts.

His words go through me like a dagger straight to the heart. It suddenly feels like I was punched in the gut, and I feel physically ill.

Jack had his way with Trinity in the woods after their near-death experience. I knew he was attracted to her. He'd said as much when we'd been alone. But I could also see it in the way he looked at her. I could see the infatuation there. Hell, I think we're all quite infatuated with her.

Sharing her with Carter was bad enough, but now to share her with Jack too...my ego is completely bruised.

I didn't think I'd be this jealous, but I've fallen for Trinity. *Hard.* I just didn't want to admit it until now.

You know the saying about love making you foolish? Well, that must be true. Because next thing I know, I'm tackling Jack to the ground and my fist is flying towards his face.

I can hear Trinity screaming for us to break it up, but I keep pummeling him. That is, until Jack gets the upper hand.

Grabbing my waist in a hold, my world suddenly turns upside down as Jack twists us and I end up under him. My face gets the brunt of his anger, and his fists feel like steel hitting bone.

I put my hands up to shield myself as Carter and Owen finally manage to pry Jack off of me. Jack stands there like a mad bull, pacing and snorting with anger. "Just remember who started it," he grits out angrily before storming off with Owen close on his heels.

I expect Trinity to run after him, but she doesn't. She falls to her knees beside me with tears in her eyes. "Lucas. Why did you do that?" she asks, her voice trembling.

"Because you're mine, Trinity."

Anger laces her features. "I'm not an object that you can just *claim*," she says, throwing our number one rule back in my face.

"I've fallen in love with you, and my jealousy got the best of me."

My words seem to stun her, and she sits quietly next to me for a long time while tears trickle down her beautiful face. "I've fallen for you too," she finally confesses.

I pull her to me, kissing her deeply and ignoring the pain that I feel…*everywhere* at the moment.

"Let's go get you cleaned up," she suggests before standing.

Carter helps me up and throws my arm around his shoulder for support as we walk up the porch steps and into the house. He settles me into one of the kitchen chairs and steps back, watching Trinity as she goes to the sink to get a wet washcloth.

Gingerly, she wipes away the blood and dirt from my face. I grimace from her ministrations, but don't say a word. I deserve the pain. I acted like a complete jealous idiot out there.

"I'll give you guys some alone time," Carter says before walking out the door.

"I'm sorry, Trinity," I tell her, grabbing her hand to halt her movement and staring into her beautiful grays.

"I'm not the one you should be apologizing to," she mutters with a small smile that tells me she's no longer totally pissed at me.

"You're right," I tell her with a nod. Then, I let go of her hand and allow her to continue cleaning me up. "I don't know what the hell got into me."

Tears fill her eyes as she bites her lower lip, and I can tell she's holding back something big.

"What is it? Tell me," I practically beg.

"Maybe this isn't going to work out between all of us," she blurts out in confession.

Squeezing my eyes shut, I shake my head slowly. "It can work. I just need to…get over my internal shit." I open my eyes and gaze up at her. Placing my palm against her soft cheek, I tell her, "If you want someone other than me, there's nothing I can do to stop you."

She leans into my touch. "I want you, Lucas." Then she says, "I was never like this before…everything happened. But this situation isn't like anything I've ever been in before. I like all of you for different and unique reasons, and I can see myself eventually falling for each one of you. I know it sounds weird…or maybe I'm just a slut —."

I cut her words off by running the pad of my thumb over her full lips. "You're not a slut, Trinity. I get it. I do. Things are different now. You're attracted to all of us?" I ask.

She gives me a nod.

"Then I'll just have to get over my internal bullshit, because I want you to be happy." I run my thumb along her soft jawline. "I just have one request."

"What's that?"

"I want you to sleep with me in my room every night. I don't want that to ever change."

She looks up at the ceiling with a thoughtful look on her face. "Well, Carter does talk in his sleep…and Jack snores pretty loud…"

I chuckle at her words and pull her close to me. "You already know I'm a good cuddle buddy."

"The best," she answers, giving me a sweet kiss.

## CHAPTER 18

*Trinity*

THE NEXT MORNING at breakfast is awkward, to say the least. Both Jack and Lucas are sporting bruises on their face, and neither one has said a single word to one another. In fact, the entire table is quiet.

Feeling beyond frustrated, I slam my fork down on the table and stand. "I don't know how much time I have left here, but I know this much — I don't want to be the cause of breaking up a great friendship." I point to Jack and then to Lucas. "You two need to squash whatever beef you have between you two and get it over with, so we can all move on."

Jack and Lucas stare at me and then look at each other before quickly looking away.

Carter stands up and says, "Trinity is right. You both threw punches, so you both need to man up and apologize."

Lucas clears his throat and nods as Carter sits back down. "I'm sorry, Jack. I don't know what the hell got into me yesterday, but I should have never attacked you."

Jack says, "And I'm sorry for breaking that beautiful face of yours."

That gets everyone around the table laughing, because Lucas looks like he was hit by a Mack truck, while Jack looks like he got away with barely a scrape.

"Totally squashed now?" Carter asks, and the two of them nod in agreement. "Good," he says with a grin, looking up at me.

I take my seat again, satisfied.

Lucas turns to me and asks, "But, Trinity, what did you mean when you said you didn't know how much time you had left here?"

Shrugging my shoulders, I take a sip of water to allow myself a minute to gather my emotions so I don't start crying all over the table. Setting down the glass, I stare down at my plate when I say, "I don't know how long you'll want to keep me here. I mean, I don't offer much. I can't even set a decent trap," I say, my voice shaking with worry.

Carter scoffs at my admission. "You do a lot around here, Trinity. You've helped all of us a lot around the farm. It takes time to learn the lay of the land, and you've done great so far." He leans across the table and gives me his famous shit-eating grin. "Besides, I don't know if you realized this or not, but we all kinda like having you around."

I look between Jack and Lucas with worry. "But what about what happened yesterday? I don't want that to happen ever again."

"It won't," Jack says simply as if that solves everything, but I believe him nonetheless.

Lucas takes his hand in mine. "We all like you Trinity, and you told me you like all of us. We want to take care of you and keep you safe."

Owen, always the quiet one, speaks up and says, "You're not leaving. You're a part of our family now."

His words have tears flooding my eyes. "You all want me to stay?"

Lucas glances around at the guys, and they all nod in confirmation. Then his eyes meet mine again. "We'd love for you to stay with us. For as long as you want to."

The idea of being shared between four men is something new to me, but it just seems right. And now that my future isn't up in the air like I thought it was, I can enjoy my time here, getting to know all of them on a personal and intimate level.

I can easily see myself falling for each and every one of them. And while that scares me a little, it thrills me more.

## CHAPTER 19

*Trinity*

OVER THE NEXT few days, I help Carter and Lucas plant and harvest in the garden and learn how to set more traps with Jack. I'm gradually getting better at everything, learning more than I ever thought possible; and spending time with each of the guys has been wonderful.

But there is still one man in my life that remains more of a mystery to me than any of them, and that's Owen. We haven't been able to spend too much time together since he's always locked away in the library or his room reading or trying to come up with a new invention that would work on the farm.

And so when he tells me after dinner that he wants to show me something in his room, I'm excited and intrigued at the same time.

I walk into his bedroom and call out, "Owen?", into the darkness.

"Over here, Trinity," he says, his voice coming from the open doors to a small balcony.

Crossing the room, I go to him. The night air is perfect — not too cold, not too warm — and I inhale it deeply, taking in the sight of the farm laid out below us. There are two balconies on this side of the house for Owen's and Carter's rooms, but Carter never seems to use his. I can see why Owen likes it out here.

It's very peaceful and calming.

"What did you want to show me?" I ask him, curiosity getting the better of me.

A grin breaks out on his face, and I feel my heart skip a beat. "Come on," he says, moving to the edge of the balcony towards the roof. There is a small rope ladder that he begins to climb. And once he's on the top, he looks down at me.

I step up, placing my feet carefully on the rope as I climb the short distance up to him. He helps me up at the top, and I fall into his chest, giggling. He immediately pulls away and flashes me a bashful look over his shoulder as he carefully walks over to the flat part of the roof. It's the highest point of the roof, surrounded by low wrought iron fencing and looks like a tiny terrace.

He has a blanket, pillows, even a telescope up here, and I can't help but wonder how long he's been planning this.

"Do you come up here often?" I ask him.

He gives me a small shrug. "Sometimes. Mostly if I can't sleep."

I hop over the fencing and sit down beside him on the blanket. "It's nice up here," I remark.

"Yeah." And then he points and says, "Look up."

I was too busy looking down that I didn't even notice the beautiful blanket of stars in the night sky above us. "Wow," I gasp. Without any lights nearby, you can see everything clearly, and it almost takes my breath away with its magnificence. "It's beautiful," I whisper.

He nods in agreement. "It is."

"Where did you find the telescope?" I ask as I watch him setting it up.

"On one of the supply runs we did a few months ago. It's my most valuable treasure now." He looks through the eyepiece, and I can almost feel the peace it brings him. "It's nice to forget about the world for a while."

He looks up and motions for me. I move over in front of him.

When I look into the eyepiece, I see a round, ochre-colored object. "Is that Mars?" I ask, glancing at him.

"Yep," he says, beaming at me proudly.

"Wow," I mutter in fascination. I'd never really been into science or space before the world took a turn for the worst, but I always found it interesting when I read articles on the internet or saw reports on the news.

He shows me the moon next and then a couple other planets. He goes through explanations and fun facts that have me captivated. He even cracks a few jokes. And by the time we get to constellations, I've fallen a little more for Owen. He's funny and sexy and oh so brilliant.

*He's irresistible.*

Once we're done star-gazing, we lay down on the blanket together, side by side.

There's not a cloud in sight, and so we can see the stars easily with the naked eye. He raises his hand and points to the brightest star in the sky. "That's Polaris, the North Star."

"At the end of the *Little Dipper*'s handle?"

He chuckles and says, "Yeah."

I may not know technical names, but I know the *Big Dipper* and *Little Dipper*.

"And there's the…*Big…Dipper*," he says the layman's term with difficulty, and it makes me laugh.

"Go ahead. You can get technical on me," I tell him.

"Okay," he says with a grin. Owen prattles off the real names of the stars — *Ursa Major*, meaning Great Bear and *Ursa Minor*, meaning Little Bear — and even gives me the Greek mythology behind both of them. Then, he moves his hand over in a different direction and tells me, "That's Hercules." He points out the stars one by one, and I get a picture in my mind of what it's supposed to look like.

I curl up beside him as he shows me star after star, constellation after constellation; his mind full of a billion facts about things I never knew about.

Leaning up on my elbow, I stare down at him as he stares at the sky. "How come you never had a girlfriend, Owen?" I ask softly.

His hazel eyes bounce from me and back to the stars. "Uh, I'm not really sure. Never had the time I guess. No one was ever really interested…or showed it anyway."

"Well, if I had met you before all of this, I would have been *very* interested," I admit to him.

He gives me a frown in response.

"What?"

"You would have never noticed me before. You're so out of my league."

I roll my eyes to the heavens. "Whatever. I am *not* out of your league."

"Yes. Yes, you are." He leans up on his elbow to match my posture. "We were thrown together in this god-awful circumstance. That's the only way I'd have a shot with someone like you."

I pick at imaginary threads on the blanket. Maybe he is right. Maybe I never would have noticed him before. But none of that matters, because we're here now. "I'll be honest, before you just confessed all of…*that*, I didn't think you even found me attractive."

"Are you kidding? God, Trinity, you're gorgeous."

I smile at his words and look up at him. "Well, it doesn't matter if we wouldn't have met in the world before this one. We're here now, aren't we?"

His dark brows furrow as he absorbs my words. "That's true. It's like the universe plucked us out of millions and millions of stars and decided to put us in the same galaxy together."

I bite back a grin. If he wants to use science analogies, then so be it. But there's something else I can think of him using his mouth for…

"Owen?"

"Yeah?" he asks.

"Just kiss me already."

With a shy grin, he leans forward and captures my mouth with his, stealing the breath right from my lungs.

His kiss is hesitant at first, but then quickly grows more heated and bolder. I didn't realize Owen would be such a good kisser, but I could stay here for hours just doing this alone. His lips are so soft.

His tongue flicks at the seam of my lips, and I open for him, giving him unfettered access to my mouth. Our tongues battle together as he moans into my mouth and runs his fingers across my cheek and into my hair.

When he pulls me closer, I can feel the growing bulge of his cock pressing against my inner thigh; and my hips involuntary jerk towards him.

He groans in response, rolling us over until he's on top of me. With my back pressing against the hard surface under the blanket, Owen takes control of the kiss, kissing me until we're both needy and breathless.

Suddenly, Owen pulls back, leaving us both panting. And it feels like forever until he finally speaks. "Trinity, I-I've never…I'm…I'm a…" he stammers nervously, meeting my gaze.

I put my fingertips to his lips and give him a reassuring smile. "It's okay, Owen. Let me take care of you," I tell him.

Pushing gently on his chest, he moves until his back is on the blanket. His eyes never leave mine as I reach to unbutton his jeans. With his help, we push the material down his legs, along with his shoes. Leaning up, he yanks his shirt up over his head in one quick move. His chest and arms are muscular, and I watch his toned abs clench as he sits up and then lies back.

"Now you're turn," he says with a sexy grin. "I want to see you, Trinity. All of you."

Standing, I slowly remove my clothes, doing a strip tease for Owen. I watch as his tongue darts out and runs over his bottom lip. His heavy cock is lying on his chiseled stomach, and it jumps when my eyes land upon it.

Running my hands over my body, I feel like some type of goddess on top of this roof under the night sky with only the stars and moon lighting up our dark universe and casting a glow over our bodies.

Owen's eyes slowly scan the length of my nakedness in a lazy perusal as he licks his plump lower lip again. I can see the heat in his gaze.

Dropping to my knees between his thighs, I take his thick length in my palm, enjoying the feeling of his hot, velvety flesh as I stroke him slowly.

His stare is searing as he watches my head lower. Opening my mouth, I take the tip of him inside of me, licking around his crown, which causes him to gasp out loud. I run my tongue down his shaft as I cup his heavy balls into my hand, kneading them softly.

While massaging his balls, I take as much of him as I can into my mouth, sucking gently and slowly.

"Oh, god, Trinity," he groans as he grabs fistfuls of the blanket into his hands.

His cock swells in my mouth as I taste him, licking, sucking and then running the edge of my teeth gently along his shaft, which causes him to hiss out a string of expletives and his hips to involuntarily lift off the blanket.

Not wanting him to finish in my mouth, I let him slip out of my mouth and then straddle his lean but powerful thighs. I run my wet slit along his length, allowing my arousal to coat him. I'm so turned on right now I can't even think straight.

"Trinity," he says, his palm pressed to my cheek and gazing into my eyes adoringly. "I'm glad I waited. And I'm happy that my first time is with you."

I smile down at him, leaning forward to kiss him sweetly. "I'm happy too," I whisper against his lips.

Sitting back, Owen's fingers find my clit, rubbing me until my arousal is dripping down my thighs. I rub myself against him, his cock hot and hard like steel between us.

Not being able to wait another second without him inside of me, I guide his cock to my entrance, sinking down on his length as he fills me inch by glorious inch.

With my hands planted on his rock-hard abs, I ride him, staring up at the stars in the night sky for a moment before my eyes drift close from the incredible feeling.

Owen's hands grip my hips, driving me down onto him harder and harder, our heavy pants the only sound in the quiet darkness.

I grind down on him with every thrust, the sensation hitting just right on my clit and bringing me ever closer to orgasm.

Owen's hand moves from my hip up to my stomach and then finally up to my breast. He pinches my pebbled nipple, creating a mixture of pleasure and pain that has me reaching the end of the abyss that much faster.

"Owen!" I cry out as the orgasm washes over me and liquid pleasure floods through my veins.

He pulls me down to him, clamping his lips down on mine, swallowing my cries. Then, he lifts his hips and drives his cock in and out of me while I lay on his chest, completely helpless to his relentless rhythm.

This new angle is hitting just the right spot inside of me, and I can feel another orgasm quickly flowing through me on the tail end of the first one. I cry out against his mouth as he holds me and consumes me.

Breaking the kiss, he cries out, "Trinity!", before pulling out and erupting between our bodies, bucking his hips one, two, three more times.

Completely exhausted, I lay there in his arms as Owen runs his fingertips over every inch of me as if he's trying to memorize my body.

I lift my head, and our eyes lock as his fingers graze down my spine. "That was incredible," he whispers before placing a sweet kiss against my forehead.

I drop my head back onto his hard chest, listening to the sound of his racing heart beat until it eventually slows, along with his breathing.

And with a smile on my face, I fall asleep in Owen's arms on the rooftop under the stars with the world in chaos all around us.

## CHAPTER 20

*Lucas*

I WAKE UP in the morning alone. I know she went to Owen's room last night. He had told me about his plan to woo Trinity under the stars on the rooftop. I guess his plan worked, because Trinity's side of my bed is cold, which can only mean one thing.

She spent the night with Owen last night.

I expect a pang of jealousy to hit me just then. But surprisingly, it doesn't. Ever since we had our little talk, I feel like everything's out in the open. It's a relief really to not feel that green little monster creeping into my mind and shading everything black around me.

I can share Trinity and be okay with it. The other guys are sharing her with *me*, after all. And I am always the one she runs to whenever she needs help or has a question. I mean that has to count for something, right?

She's extremely important to me, priority number one, and I know she feels the same way about me.

That's all that really matters.

After a shower, I go downstairs to find everyone in the kitchen, eating breakfast. Owen has a permanent, goofy grin on his face. And instead of feeling angry or resentful towards him, I'm actually happy that he finally got laid.

Owen had confessed to me a few months back that he'd never slept with a girl. And he truly didn't think he ever would, since the world went to hell in a handbasket.

So, I'm glad the guy finally got to experience something he should have a long time ago.

After breakfast, we all go our separate ways. I feed the animals and keep myself busy collecting eggs and milk.

And when I go into the house later that afternoon, I find Trinity sitting by the window in the living room. She has a bag of old beads and string in her hand, and she's making some type of jewelry. She looks so relaxed and…so damn perfect.

I walk over to her and plant a kiss to the top of her head. "I missed you in my bed last night," I confess, sitting down across from her.

She slips another bead onto the string before cutting the end with a pair of scissors. "Jealous?" she asks hesitantly, her eyes looking up to search my face for clues.

"A little," I admit. "But I'll get over it," I assure her.

She gives me a relieved smile.

"I'm glad you were Owen's first," I whisper just in case he's near.

Her smile widens. "I'm glad too," she confesses. And then I watch as she ties the end of the string and slips the beaded necklace around her neck. "Do you like it?" she asks, gesturing towards her creation.

"It's perfect. Just like you."

She hops up from her chair and sits down on my lap, wrapping her arms around my neck. "How did I get so lucky to find a house full of hot, gorgeous, wonderful men?"

"We're the lucky ones," I tell her, pulling her in for a deep, wet kiss.

When I pull back, I trail my fingers along the stitches on her forehead. "These are ready to come out."

"Will it hurt?" she asks, biting her lower lip, which drives me crazy.

"Don't worry. I'll make you feel all better afterwards."

Standing up and lifting her up in my arms at the same time, she squeals in surprise and then laughs. It's a melodic sound that I could listen to for the rest of my life.

And I plan on doing just that.

## CHAPTER 21

*Trinity*

LUCAS AND I are lying in bed, talking softly to one another in the dark, when suddenly the ceiling light flickers. We both sit up in surprise and stare at the bulb as it flickers again and then stays on.

"Holy shit, it worked," Lucas mutters incredulously under his breath. "He did it."

I can't help the big smile that spreads across my face in what can only be described as pure, undiluted pride. Owen has been working on perfecting a wind turbine for a while now, and he had been trying to figure out the wiring to the house that would be safe and efficient.

Lucas turns to me, and we share an unspoken agreement. We both bound out of bed and race down the stairs. Jack and Carter are already there, patting Owen on the back and congratulating him.

Owen fixes his dark-rimmed glasses, runs a hand through his haphazard hair and gives me a shy smile.

"Wow, Owen, you really did it," I say, walking up to him and planting a big kiss on his lips.

The rest of the guys catcall and whistle around us. And when I pull back, Owen looks stunned and even more disheveled.

"If I had known turning on the lights would earn me a kiss like that, I would have tried harder to get it done sooner," he says with a sexy, crooked grin.

Jack playfully ruffles his hair and slaps him on the back, nearly knocking his glasses right off his face. I bite back a chuckle as I watch the two of them interact. I think in a lot of ways Jack likes to think of Owen as the little brother he never had.

"Well, there's no way I'm sleeping now," Carter announces. "Poker?"

Usually he's the only one that wants to play, but tonight we're all wired and anxious to do something under real light instead of candlelight.

We play poker into the wee hours of the night, and it's nice to actually be able to see all my cards and everyone's tells.

For instance, Jack always frowns when he has a bad hand. Otherwise, his face stays solid like stone.

And the corner of Carter's mouth lifts in a sexy way when he's bluffing.

Lucas scratches his head when he has a bad hand and is ready to fold.

And Owen licks his lips when he's about to win the whole pot.

All of them are so different, and yet I love all of them equally the same. I never thought it would be possible to love four men at the same time.

But as we sit in our farmhouse kitchen, playing poker under bright lights with electricity buzzing all around us in an apocalyptic world, I begin to believe that anything is possible.

## CHAPTER 22

*Trinity*

THE GUYS TELL me the next morning to not come into the equipment barn because they're working on a surprise for me. I wish they wouldn't have told me that, though, because it only makes me even more curious to know what they're up to.

But I give them space...or at least try to anyway, only peeking towards the barn every few minutes or so while they work diligently on something inside.

When I finish with my chores that afternoon, I take a hot shower. The water feels so good running over my sore muscles. Life on the farm is no joke. I've been working muscles I didn't even know I had prior to arriving here.

After the shower, I dry off and step into Lucas's room. Laid out on the bed is a sundress, and I smile. He must have found it in one of the boxes of clothes. It's a little wrinkled, but it's so pretty that a wrinkle or two won't even matter.

I pull the soft material over my head and slip the spaghetti straps over my tanned shoulders. It's very pretty. The dress is white with pastel flowers all over it. The skirt of the dress hits mid-thigh, and it's flowy and flirty. I twirl a little bit in front of the large mirror on top of the old dresser.

I'm mid-twirl when I spot Lucas in the reflection behind me, standing in the doorway with a big grin on his face. His eyes lazily peruse my body until they come back up to meet mine. "You look beautiful, Trin."

I notice that he's dressed up as well in black pants and a button-down white shirt with the sleeves rolled up to show off his muscular forearms.

"You don't look too bad yourself," I tell him with a wink.

His grin widens, and he comes over to pull me into his arms. His lips instantly meet mine, and my knees go weak. He kisses me gently at first, but like always, our kiss turns heated.

He reluctantly pulls away with a groan. "Fuck, I told the guys I was coming to get you, but now I just want you all to myself."

I giggle at his words and place my palm against his warm cheek. His day-old stubble feels prickly against my skin. "There's always time for us...later," I say, motioning to the bed.

He bites his lower lip and shakes his head. "Naughty girl." In a swift motion, he turns me in his arms, captures my hand in his and twirls me out before pulling me back to him. Then, he slowly sways with me in his arms to music only he can hear in his head. "Save a dance for me tonight, okay?"

I liquefy at his words. *If only we had some* real *music...* It feels like ages since I've heard music.

He pulls away from me then and motions towards the door. "If we don't show up soon, they'll send Carter after us." When I walk past him, he swats me on the ass. Hard.

I look back at him and can't help but laugh at the devilish grin on his face. I don't know what the guys have planned for me tonight, but if this is a preview...then I'm in trouble.

Lucas and I walk hand in hand to the barn, and he only releases me to open the door. This barn is the one that Lucas, Carter and I had our first tryst together in, and I'm instantly flooded with sinful memories of our threesome that still makes me hot whenever I think about that day.

"I hope you're hungry," Lucas whispers in my ear.

"Famished," I answer.

This is the barn that is used for storing equipment, so I have no idea how we'd be eating dinner in here...unless it's on top of a tractor.

But when Lucas opens the door fully, I'm so taken aback that I'm speechless at the sight before me.

The barn has been cleaned up — the farm equipment moved to the back corner, and tiny, white Christmas lights strung up throughout the big space. A large table sits in the middle complete with placemats, a fancy table runner and fine china that they must have found somewhere in the house. There is a smorgasbord of food sitting in the center of the table — roasted chicken, mashed potatoes, corn, even gravy and homemade biscuits. And best of all? Three bottles of wine.

My mouth waters instantly at the sight, and I still can't talk because I'm so overwhelmed that they went to all this trouble for me.

Tears fill my eyes as I look at each one of them. They're all cleaned up and dressed in the nicest clothes they own, and I place my palm over my heart that's threatening to jump right out of my chest.

"Uh-oh, she's speechless." Carter says. "I think we broke her."

I release a half sob, half chuckle and say, "This is wonderful. Thank you all so much...for all of this."

"Just wait 'til dessert," Carter says with a wink.

*Dessert?*

Before I can even ponder about what delicious concoction he came up with, Lucas guides me to the table. I take a seat, and then all of my guys do as well. We waste no time digging into the meal that tastes just as delicious as it looks.

As the guys talk about tonight's preparations, I realize each one of them had their own part in it. Lucas harvested the food; Carter cooked the meal; Jack moved the equipment and cleaned up; and Owen rigged the electricity to the barn. They all helped hanging the lights, which are twinkling high above us and creating our own version of an indoor night sky.

I take a sip of the wine that Carter says he found on one of their supply runs. "I've been saving it for a rainy day," he tells me.

Well, I'm glad he chose tonight to finally crack the bottles open. The wine tastes absolutely delicious, and I have to stop myself from downing it in one swig.

With our bellies full and our heads a little lightheaded from the alcohol, we relax back in our chairs and talk about life before the apocalypse for a while, reminiscing over fond memories of our loved ones and days spent not hiding in fear of the unknown.

When we reach the point of comfortable silence, Carter says, "Time for your next surprise."

I cock my head and watch as he walks over to an old boom box on a small table. And when he hits a few buttons and soft music begins to pour out of the speakers, I'm struck speechless again.

It's an old country tune, but to me it's the most beautiful thing I have ever heard. Jumping out of my seat, I run over to him excitedly.

He smiles down at me as I check out the radio. "Could only find some old country tapes and CDs. I was really looking forward to listening to some Def Leppard or Ozzy, but no such luck," he says with a frown.

I chuckle and trail my finger along the dusty boom box. "This is… this is perfect," I say, beaming up at him.

"Dance with me, Trinity," he leans down to whisper into my ear, and it sends a shiver through me.

Pulling me into his arms, we sway gently to the music. It feels so weird to be doing something that was considered to be so *normal* back then.

"God, we really didn't know how good we had it before the apocalypse, did we?" I ask, my voice full of sadness.

"No. No, we didn't," he agrees, pulling me impossibly closer.

I rest my head on his chest, listening to his heart beat in tune with the music. After a while, Jack cuts in, wanting to dance with me. I fall into his giant, muscular arms and have to hold back a laugh when I realize he's the only one wearing cut off sleeves because he couldn't find a nice dress shirt with sleeves big enough to hold all of his large muscles.

Jack holds me as if I'm made of glass, only confirming his title of being a giant teddy bear, and the warmth coming from his bare skin feels so good, warming me to my very core.

Next to cut in is Owen. He's unsure of how to hold me and then immediately confesses that he doesn't know how to dance. So, I decide to put him out of his misery and take over to lead, telling him to stop worrying so much and to just go with the flow. Eventually, he starts to relax from that stiff-as-a-board state he was in and actually begins enjoying himself, even leading me around our makeshift dance floor.

We dance to a few songs before I see Lucas in my periphery. He's been watching me dance with everyone else with longing written all over his face. When he finally tugs me into his arms, I look up at his handsome face and can't help but smile. "Now I know what you meant when you said earlier to save you a dance."

"I didn't want to ruin the surprise," he says softly. "Fuck, you look so beautiful tonight, Trin. Especially in that dress."

I wrap my hands around his neck and pull him down to me, his lips meeting mine in a passionate kiss. He tastes like sweet wine, and I can't get enough.

Like all the other times we kiss, the world around us begins to melt, and we are the only two that exist in our own little bubble.

It isn't until I feel a warm body sliding up behind me that it hits me that we're not alone. Carter turns me so that my front is pressed up against him and my backside is pressed up against Lucas. And then, he gently grips my chin and tilts my head up so that my lips meet his in a soul-searing kiss.

While Carter devours me, Lucas's hands roam all over my body, my breasts, my hips, my ass before cupping my cheeks hard and pulling me tight up against him. The evidence of his arousal pushes deep into my backside, and I gasp loudly.

Carter's lips move over my jaw and then to my neck, licking and biting gently as I throw my head back to rest on Lucas's chest.

With me sandwiched between them, they have their way with me, grinding their thickening lengths against me while their hands wander over my body.

Suddenly, Carter grabs the hem of my dress and tugs it up my thighs. And with Lucas's help, they pull it up over my head.

With no bra or panties on, I'm completely bared to them. But I don't feel exposed.

*I feel free.*

"Fuck, you're gorgeous," Carter whispers against my neck before he lightly nips at my skin and then soothes the bite with his talented tongue. His mouth moves lower, trailing down my neck to my breast where he sucks on my pebbled nipple, taking it into his warm mouth and sucking until I'm aching with need.

While Carter's attention is on my breasts, Lucas's adept fingers dip between my legs, finding my already wet seam. He groans against my hair as he slips a finger inside of me, pumping in and out so slowly.

"All of us want you tonight, Trin," Lucas whispers into my ear. "But the question is…do you want all of us…all at the same time?"

I only hesitate a moment before I moan out a yes.

I hadn't really ever thought of having them all inside of me at the same time, but right now I'm so turned on that the idea of them all touching me, kissing me, licking me, fucking me that it almost sends me right into an orgasm.

Carter releases my nipple from his mouth with a *pop* and gazes up at me. "I think it's time for dessert," Carter says with a mischievous grin.

"Dessert?" I ask in a lust-induced fog.

"Oh, we're definitely hungry for that dessert. In fact, I'm practically starving."

When Carter leads me over to the table, which has now been cleared off thanks to Jack and Owen, I realize then that the dessert he promised might not be something to eat, after all. I think *I'm* the dessert.

Carter strips out of his shirt, revealing his muscular chest littered with tattoos. He rolls his shirt in his hands and then gently places it over my eyes, tying the sleeves in the back to create an improvised blindfold.

"Don't take it off, gorgeous," he whispers into my ear, sending a shiver through me.

I realize I'm standing naked before all four of my guys...who I can't even see at the moment.

Feeling self-conscious, I try to hide myself, but Carter takes my hands in his and scolds me by clicking his tongue. "You're too beautiful to hide. We all want to see you."

His hands gently guide me to the table behind us, and he coaxes me to lay face down. I press my front into the hard wood and turn my head to the side, my breaths coming out in rapid pants as I wait in anticipation for what will come next.

But my brain couldn't have even fathomed what happened next, because it's the most erotic and incredible thing I've ever experienced.

With a few strange sounds that sound like bottles opening and then the smell of strawberries wafting through the air, I feel the first pair of hands on me, followed closely behind by three more pairs.

A sweet-smelling oil is slickened over my entire backside as the hands massage the liquid into my skin. My muscles melt under their touch, and I try to pinpoint exactly whose hands are where on my body.

Jack is cocksure, no hesitation whatsoever, rubbing over my legs while Owen is hesitant but then steady as he massages my back. Carter's hands are calloused from all the work he does with his hands, so I feel him rubbing oil over my ass, squeezing my cheeks for good measure. And Lucas's are soft, gentle, teasing as he works my neck and arms.

They work the oil into every crack and crevice, and I can feel Carter's hands dip in between my legs, working against my clit. And then someone else begins to massage my back entrance, dipping an oiled fingertip into the forbidden place.

I gasp out loudly at the sensation. I've never taken a man there before. I've always been terrified of it hurting too badly.

"Have you ever let a man fuck you here before?" Lucas asks.

I shake my head, unable to say the words out loud.

But as Lucas's fingers prod inside of me as Carter works my clit, the sensation is incredible, and I find myself crying out, not for them to stop, but for more.

My body begins to quiver with need beneath their hands, and I can't even stop myself when I suddenly beg, "Please!"

Jack chuckles darkly at my plea. "Please what, Trinity?" he whispers by my ear.

"Please...fuck me," I plead, my voice needy and desperate with lust.

The hands suddenly stop their ministrations, and then I'm turned over onto my back and slid to the end of the table. My legs dangle over the edge before they're captured in someone's hands. The warm hands gently spread me apart, and I sink my teeth into my bottom lip as I realize I'm wide open for everyone to see.

It should scare me. But I'm so turned on and my brain is so foggy with lust that I can't even think about anything other than feeling all of their hands on me again.

"I'm ready for my dessert now, Trinity," Carter says before diving in between my thighs like a starving man. His talented tongue laps furiously between my legs, driving me absolutely crazy with need.

As Carter devours me, someone cups my right breast before dragging his teeth against the stiff peak. I cry out at the combined sensations. And when someone else sucks my other nipple into his hot mouth, my back arches off the table from the overwhelming sense of being touched *everywhere* all at the same time.

With one of my senses dulled, the other ones seem to come alive. I feel *everything* — every little touch, every lick, pinch, bite.

I hear the table creak beside my head, and then someone stretches my arms above my head, his large hand shackling my wrists. A moment later, I feel the soft, warm skin of his rock-hard cock sliding across my lips.

"Open up for me, Trin," Lucas's rugged voice rasps.

My lips part, and my tongue darts out as I lick around his crown, earning me a low, primal groan that vibrates through my entire body.

Lucas slowly eases his fingers into my hair, holding me in place as he drives his cock into my wet mouth. I take him into my mouth, tasting his clean scent and loving the way his velvety steel feels against my tongue. I swallow deep, taking him as far as I can down my throat, gagging on his girth.

"That's my girl," he groans. "Everyone is watching you, Trin. You're so fucking beautiful with my cock in your mouth."

My chest and cheeks flush instantly at his words, and I'm suddenly glad for the blindfold. I can see now the reasoning behind it as well. They wanted me to start off in a small pond before jumping into a lake. Too much too soon would have made me feel shy and vulnerable. But blocking off my sense of sight has opened my mind up to new possibilities. New possibilities involving *all* of my men…at the same time.

Carter's hot, wet tongue circles on the swollen little bundle of nerves, and I moan around Lucas's cock, trying not to scream.

"That's it, Trin," Lucas hisses. "Come for us."

That seems to fuel Carter on, because he wraps his hands around my hips, holding me in place as he devours me, licking me into oblivion. I cry out around Lucas's steel length, sucking him hard and shuddering as waves of pleasure crash over me again and again.

With my brain swimming in a fog of endorphins, I barely even notice when Lucas pulls his cock out of my mouth and the blindfold suddenly disappears.

Blinking up at the tiny lights strung up above me, my four guys all look down at me with greedy, lust-filled gazes as Carter says, "I hope you're ready for more."

He helps me off the table only to turn me around and press me down onto the hard wood. My hands stretch out beside me as my head swirls with lust.

Carter teases my slit with his cock, rubbing the head over my clit all the way to my entrance and back again. My legs quiver with need as my fingernails dig into the wood.

"Please!" I beg him.

I'm rewarded with his dark chuckle as he pushes just the head of his cock into me. With shallow, short thrusts, he teases all my nerve endings, driving me up the wall with the need to have him deep inside of me.

I try to thrust my hips back into him, but he counters my move every damn time.

Leaning over my back, he whispers into my ear, "I want to hear you beg me for my cock, Trinity."

Without any hesitation, I cry out, "Please, Carter! Please fuck me. Fuck me, please." I'm a quivering mess, and tears fill my eyes as he continues to tease me.

And when he finally rocks into me, thrusting brutally into my pussy, he feels so fucking good buried deep inside of me that I cry out in relief.

Sheathing himself into my warmth, he thrusts into me, hitting the sweet spot deep inside me that has me climbing towards another release at a rapid pace.

Glancing over at Jack, Owen and Lucas, I see their cocks are hard and practically weeping for me with beads of pre-cum spilling over their crowns as they stroke themselves.

Jack comes closer and wraps my hand around his thick cock. I stroke him gently while Carter claims me from behind, his hard cock filling the depths of my pussy.

Jack's hips jerk towards me as I stroke his length faster, my fingertips now and then caressing his heavy balls, causing him to groan low and deep.

As Owen approaches, Carter pulls my back against his chest, capturing me in his strong arms. Owen lavishes my breasts, sucking my nipples into his warm, wet mouth.

All of it is too much to take, and I find myself tumbling over the edge, my tight channel clamping down on Carter's length. My eyes roll to the back of my head as the orgasm rips through me, destroying me with every shudder and quiver.

## CHAPTER 23

*Lucas*

FUCK, I NEED *to be inside of her.*

That's the only thing I can think of as I climb down from the table. My cock is as hard as steel, bobbing between my thighs. And when I watch Carter bend Trinity over the table and slide his dick inside of her, her lithe body writhing underneath him, I grow impossibly harder.

Palming my shaft, I stroke slowly as I watch the two of them fuck. My cock pulses with want as a clear bead of precum drips from the tip. It's practically begging to be inside of her.

I watch as Jack walks up to the table and wraps Trinity's hand around his cock, and she strokes him gently. He throws his head back and murmurs a curse.

Then, Carter pulls Trinity back against his chest, his arms possessively wrapped around her waist and neck as Owen runs his hands over Trinity's breasts, tugging on her pale, pink nipples before lavishing them with his tongue.

Trinity's moans grow louder and more desperate, and it's music to my fucking ears.

I don't know how we all came to a plan for tonight. It all started off with Carter being the smartass he always is and saying about how it would be hot if we all fucked her together. At first, we laughed it off, dismissing the idea. But as soon as his idea was planted in our minds, it rooted itself and grew until it was all we could talk about when Trinity wasn't around.

The thought of all of us taking her at the same time turned us on to no end. We wanted to wait for the perfect opportunity and treat her right, give her more pleasure than she's ever had in her life.

And so far, our plan is working.

Trinity's eyes are hooded as she cries out through a second orgasm thanks to Carter's cock. He pulls out of her as he reaches his own bliss, coating her skin with his seed.

"Fuck," he groans under his breath before turning her head to steal a kiss from her. "You're so gorgeous when you're coming on my cock," he whispers to her.

Once he steps away, I walk over to Trinity and lead her over to a low bench. I lay down, bringing her with me to straddle my thighs. She smiles down at me; and in that moment, she's so fucking beautiful it physically hurts to look at her.

Unable to resist any longer, I pull her to me, kissing her sweetly, gently.

"I need to be inside of you," I growl in a whisper against her bee-stung lips.

She places her small hand on my hard chest as she lines her entrance up with my cock and sinks down until she's fully seated.

And, fuck, it feels like heaven.

She works her hips, grinding down on me. "Oh fuck," I moan, gripping her hips in a bruising hold. I stare into her beautiful, stormy, gray eyes as she rides me at a slow and languid pace, driving me fucking crazy.

Jack stands behind her, massaging her ass and testing her readiness with his fingers easing in and out of her tight asshole gently. Trinity gasps and moans out loud as he prods her back entrance.

When he gives me a nod, I curve an arm around Trinity's back and pull her flat to my chest, presenting her luscious ass to Jack, so that he can claim it.

His cock eases in, and he's careful not go to too fast, allowing her to stretch for him as I thrust my hips up and grind myself against her clit. Her quick breaths fall against my neck as I hold her to me, rubbing my hands along her back while Jack continues to drive himself into her.

"Oh god, oh god, oh god," Trinity whispers against my skin. She's panting, working hard and getting both of her holes filled at the same fucking time.

An animalistic sound vibrates in Jack's throat when he finally buries his cock to the hilt. Rocking gently back and forth, we fuck Trinity in unison, both taking what we want and giving her exactly what she fucking needs.

We move together in a fluid motion like waves crashing over the shore, our pleasure climbing to new heights.

Trinity cries out nonsensical things, biting into my shoulder to keep from screaming out. Her teeth sinking into my skin adds a shred of pain to the experience and brings me even closer to the edge.

Her thighs quiver as we take her. Her liquid heat coats my length as I pound into her with vicious thrusts, eliciting the sweetest moans from her.

Owen, the shy guy he is, finally steps up to the plate, and I guide Trinity's mouth to his waiting cock. I think he enjoyed watching us, however. Trinity told me how he watched me fucking her in the kitchen that one day. I was surprised to learn that the nerdy science boy has a kinky side.

I watch as she sucks his cock, licking down his length and back up again. Owen's eyes fall closed as he enjoys every single second of the pleasure she's giving him.

Fuck, I know exactly how he feels.

Everything Trinity does feels so damn good. It's like her body was made for fucking.

Trinity's body bucks under my grip as she cries out around Owen's cock with an earth-shattering orgasm.

Jack is quick to follow, exploding inside of her with a loud roar that threatens to shake down the barn's walls. He buries himself into her one last time, cursing under his breath as he plants kisses along her spine.

Jack slowly pulls out, leaving Owen and me the last men standing. Owen threads his fingers through Trinity's hair, drawing her down on his cock time and time again until he's groaning through his orgasm and coating her tongue with his release.

Owen then staggers over to join the rest of them over by the table, and I'm happy to have some alone time with Trinity...even though we're in a room full of people who are watching us.

Sitting up straight with her in my lap, her entire body shudders as I viciously piston my hips, driving my length up into her. Every time with her is incredible, and I know I'll never be able to get enough of her.

Trinity suddenly calls out my name as another orgasm rips through her. And as her muscles clench around me like a damn vice, I can feel my release building at the base of my spine and tightening in my balls.

The tension slowly keeps building until finally I go over the edge brutally, holding her to me tightly. Her inner walls contract around my cock, squeezing and milking me as I come inside of her, coating her inner walls with my release, and the feeling is fucking incredible.

Trinity collapses against my chest, exhausted as I stroke her back, whispering soothing praises into her ear.

I know I should have pulled out, because that was definitely *not* part of our plan. But when I think of Trinity pregnant with my child, it fills me with an overwhelming sense of pride and joy.

I'm sure it will be something we'll have to sit down and discuss at some point, but right now I want to revel in the fact that I claimed her as mine the only way I knew how.

## CHAPTER 24

*Carter*

IT'S LATE AT night...or early in the morning, depending on how you look at it. I'm sitting at the kitchen table in the dark, nursing the last glass of wine when I hear the stairs creak.

I expect it to be Jack or maybe even Lucas, but imagine my surprise when Trinity emerges from the shadows.

"You're still up," she says observantly.

I quickly take in her appearance. Her beautiful, long legs are sticking out from under a dress shirt she must have borrowed from one of us. And fuck, I wish I could claim that it was mine, but it's most likely Lucas's since she just came down from his room.

It pissed me off in the beginning that she always wanted to sleep with Lucas, but I've since gotten over it. I mean, he did kind of claim her since she first arrived by putting her in his room to begin with.

And earlier, he was the first to come in her beautiful pussy. Now I can't say that that didn't piss me off, because I was downright furious with him afterwards. I think we all were.

We don't have many rules, and we sure as shit didn't fully plan the big fuck-fest that took place just hours ago, but I thought we could trust each other to not claim her with everyone else present.

There is the risk of her getting pregnant, but for some reason it doesn't terrify me like it would have in my past. No, the thought of Trinity being barefoot and pregnant turns me the fuck on.

Stalking over to her, I capture her against the wall, slowly caging her in with my arms. "Why couldn't you sleep?" I ask in a hushed voice.

"I was thirsty," she whispers back. "Why couldn't you sleep?" she asks, repeating my question.

"I guess I was hungry. But I didn't realize how hungry I was until you came downstairs," I tell her before crashing my mouth down on hers. Our kiss is ravenous and all-consuming. My tongue forces its way into her mouth, possessing her...claiming her...owning her.

She whimpers into my mouth, and I swallow down her cries.

Her hips buck against me, and I know exactly what my girl wants. My fingertips find her wet slit, and it makes the monster inside me roar that she's already wet for me. I tease her clit until her nails are clawing at my back and she's begging me to fuck her.

And even though I just had her hours prior, I want her again...and again...and again. I'll never get my fill of this girl no matter how many times I take her, and that drives me fucking crazy.

Pulling down my sweatpants to my hips, I release my erection, which bobs up towards my abs. I lift her in my arms, pinning her against the kitchen wall with my hips. Grabbing myself at the root, I guide her pussy onto my cock, pushing in achingly slow and wanting to make the moment last as long as it possibly can.

Her nails rake along my back again as I take my time fucking her, relishing in the warmth of her pussy sheathing my hard cock and her tight channel pulsing around me.

The bite of her nails has me hissing through clenched teeth. Fuck, I'm gonna look like I got into a fight with a wildcat tomorrow. But I can't fucking wait to show the guys and brag to them about how I fucked her tight, little pussy while they were all in bed, asleep.

My fingertips dig into her ass cheeks as I take what's mine, pistoning my hips faster and faster until she's crying out as I drive myself right into her sweet spot.

I stare down at our connection and watch my dick stretching her to the brim. "Fuck, that's hot," I groan.

Trinity grinds her hips down onto my cock, trying to find her release as she clings to my shoulders. "Please, please, please, please," she begs against my neck.

I speed up my thrusts, rutting in and out of her like a wild animal, my grunts feral. "Come for me, Trinity," I demand.

And as if my words somehow conjured her pleasure, she detonates around me, quivering in my arms as she whimpers through a powerful orgasm.

I pound up into her, loving the way her tight pussy grips me and clamps down like a vice with the aftershocks of her orgasm. My cock pulses and grows inside of her as my balls tighten and a sharp shock of pleasure runs down my spine.

"Oh, fuck!" I cry out before I empty myself inside of her, my warm release coating her tight channel.

We stand there for a while with her in my arms and me pinning her against the wall until my cock slowly softens and our breathing finally evens out.

I pull out of her then, and she lowers her legs to the floor, but I still can't let her go. I stare down at her beautiful face and kiss her sweetly, softly.

"Wait here," I tell her before running to grab a cloth. I run the water in the sink until it's warm and then wet the cloth before returning to Trinity. I go to my knees in front of her and gently wipe between her legs until the evidence of our lovemaking is gone.

Looking up at her, a smile graces my lips when I realize I fucked her while she was wearing Lucas's shirt. He's gonna be pissed, but I guess we're even now.

I wipe off my cock before pulling up my sweatpants and throwing the cloth onto the pile of dirty clothes that I'll take care of tomorrow.

"I'm going to get a glass of water before I head back to bed," Trinity tells me.

I give her a chaste kiss and tell her, "Okay. I'll see you tomorrow, beautiful. Goodnight."

"Goodnight," she whispers back.

I leave the kitchen and almost run smack-dab into Owen. "Jesus," I say, grabbing my heart in overdramatic fashion. "You scared the fuck out of me. What are you doing standing in the dark like that?"

When he starts stammering through an excuse, realization slowly dawns on me — he was watching the two of us fuck. "Were you just —?"

He gives me a sheepish grin, and then I know for sure.

"Fucking voyeur," I say with a chuckle and a shake of my head. I clap him on the shoulder and head up to bed with a smile on my face.

## CHAPTER 25

*Trinity*

THE NEXT MORNING I wake up late and with a smile on my face. I slept like a baby. But after what happened last night, it's no wonder.

But my happiness is short-lived when I go downstairs to find Jack, Owen and Carter out on the front porch gearing up for something. And the way they're clipping knives and guns onto themselves, it makes me think it's something very dangerous.

Lucas is by the sink, rinsing out a cup when he turns to see me. "Hey, sleepyhead," he says affectionately.

"Where are they going?" I ask nervously.

"They're going on a supply run," Lucas explains. He runs a hand through his hair that's still damp from his shower. "I volunteered to stay behind with you."

"But aren't supply runs dangerous?"

He shrugs and says, "Yeah, but, I mean, we have to do it. It's just the way of life now."

I stare out the window, watching them getting ready. And I can't help but feel a pang of hurt and worry in my chest that just won't go away. What if they get hurt? What if they don't come back? A million different scenarios are running through my head.

I'd been so focused on the front porch that I don't even see or hear Lucas approach until he's wrapping his arms around me. "They're gonna be fine, Trin. We've all gone on plenty of supply runs before. I'm sure they'll be careful."

I give him a small nod, although I can't stop the queasy feeling in my stomach.

As I walk out on the porch, the guys all turn to look at me. None of them look worried, and it puts me at ease. Somewhat.

I take turns hugging and kissing each one of them individually, whispering in their ears to come back home to me. I've grown to love my men, and I can't bear the thought of anything bad happening to any one of them.

A little while later, Lucas and I are standing on the front porch, watching the three of them take off in an old truck down the driveway, stopping to open the gate and then disappearing out into the world.

A shiver runs through as I think about every little thing that could happen to them while they're gone.

Lucas puts his arm around me and pulls me close for a side hug. "They'll be back before you know it, Trin. I promise." Kissing the top of my head, he pulls back and asks, "Do you want to work on the garden today while I feed the animals? It will help keep us busy until they get back."

"Yeah," I tell him, because a distraction right now is exactly what I need. Otherwise, I might worry myself to death until they return.

# CHAPTER 26

*Owen*

I'VE NEVER BEEN around a beautiful woman like Trinity before. She's so distracting that she makes me forget about everything I'm working on or want to work on…or have worked on, for that matter, whenever she's near.

I calculated the odds of her stumbling upon our farm, and let's just say that, mathematically speaking, it's a borderline miracle.

Our group was solid before, but I think we've become a force to be reckoned with since her arrival. Even I find myself wanting to work out more with Jack. Although, I could never keep up with his strict and brutal regimen. But the truth of the matter is I actually want to *try*, and that's something I really had no desire for before Trinity arrived.

We all want to be our best around her and the best for her, to protect her.

In the short time she's been here, she's managed to put us all under the same spell. And I for one can say I'm completely smitten.

Growing up as the nerdy science geek, I never really had friends, and I certainly never had girlfriends. I had friends that were girls, but

I was always held back in the friend zone while they made out with their popular, jock boyfriends and went to dances without me.

I was bullied mercilessly all through school, but I think in a way it made me who I am today.

I wanted to get the hell out of school, so I pushed myself, academically speaking. I graduated from high school at the ripe old age of fourteen and went straight to college. Several years later, I had a Ph.D. under my belt and something to feel proud of.

With a successful and busy career, my love life was put completely on the backburner. I never had time for relationships, but it's not like women were waiting in line or anything to date me.

And then, when the apocalypse hit, I truly never thought I would meet anyone special in my life. Never find *the one*.

Never lose my virginity. That's for sure.

Those things used to depress me and keep me up at night.

But what I didn't know was that the universe had a plan for me all along. Trinity turned my entire world upside down just when I had lost all hope. And when I made love to her for the first time, I knew I wanted to experience that again and again with her.

She's the one I want to be a better man for now. She makes me want to be a better person.

As we cruise down the empty and forgotten highway, I miss her terribly. She has become very important to me in such a short time, and I hope she stays with us. Forever.

And so when Carter asks me if I want to go anywhere special today on our supply run, I instantly tell him, "A library," before pushing my glasses up the bridge of my nose.

There's a specific book that I want to find for my girl, and I can't wait to see her face when I bring it home for her.

## CHAPTER 27

*Lucas*

AFTER I'M FINISHED feeding the animals and giving them water, my stomach rumbles loudly, echoing in the barn. Feeling famished, I decide to go see if Trinity is ready for some lunch.

Exiting the barn, I lock the doors up tight.

Staring off in the distance, I see Trinity bent over, weeding in the garden. The way her ass moves around makes my cock twitch.

Even though we've fucked almost every night she's been in my bed, I just can't get enough of her. And now that the guys are gone today, my mind starts thinking of all the ways I could dirty her up… on every surface of the house.

My cock jumps in my pants, straining against the material, begging to be let free. "Down boy," I whisper.

Grabbing the empty water bucket, I double-check the locks on the barn before walking towards the garden.

Suddenly, I feel an intense pain in the back of my head. I blink, and I'm falling to the ground. I blink again, and I'm sprawled out on the grass.

"Fffuucckkk," I drawl out groggily, not knowing what the hell just happened. I touch the back of my head and my fingers come back covered in blood. *Was I shot?*

Through blurry vision I see a figure appear at my side. The man is haggard with long, matted brown hair and crazy, dark eyes. His clothes are dirty and torn, and his feet are bare and covered in blood and mud.

And then I spot the shovel in his hand and can only reach one conclusion in my foggy brain. He snuck up on me and hit me in the back of the head with the damn thing.

"Where is she?" he hisses at me, dropping the shovel and brandishing a large knife.

"Who...who are you?" I manage to croak out.

"Doesn't matter who I am. Where. Is. She?" he asks, enunciating each word.

I open my mouth to tell him to go fuck off, but the dark fog in my brain begins to pull me under, and it suddenly feels like I'm drowning.

The last thought I have is that I've left Trinity unprotected against this mad man and that I may never see her beautiful face again.

## CHAPTER 28

*Trinity*

WHILE LUCAS FEEDS the animals, I busy myself in the garden. I'd do anything at this point to keep my mind off the fact that the rest of the guys are currently risking their lives on a supply run. Just the thought of one...or all of them...not making it back makes me physically ill.

And so I keep my hands busy and try to keep my mind from straying to the horrible possibilities that could occur today.

I'm so distracted that I don't even hear Lucas's footsteps until his shadow casts over me. With a smile on my face, I stand and turn towards him.

But my smile instantly fades when I realize Lucas isn't standing there, but instead there's a strange man. I take a step back, ice crystallizing in my veins with terror.

"Hello, Trinity," the man rasps out in an eerily familiar voice.

I gasp, almost not recognizing the person in front of me. "Henry?" I question in disbelief. He's covered in dirt and his beard and hair have grown long and scraggly. But the crazed look in his eye is what gives me pause the most. "What are you..." My voice trails off as my eyes zero in on the knife in his hand. A knife that's covered in dried blood. My mind races as I begin to wonder if that's Lucas's blood or not. "What did you do, Henry?" I whisper.

"What I had to," he says enigmatically.

Did he hurt Lucas? Is Lucas even still alive? I have to go to him. I try to run past Henry, but he reaches out and grabs me from behind, pulling my back to his front in an unrelenting grip.

"You're not going anywhere!" he hisses in my ear.

I struggle against him, fighting with all my might, but he's insanely strong. My shoes tear into the ground below me as we struggle. But when I feel the cold steel of the blade pressed up against my neck, all my fight instantly flees my body.

"Don't make me hurt you, Trinity," he says, desperation lacing his voice. "I came all this way for you, and I'm not leaving without you."

I go pliant in his hold. "Okay, okay. I'll go with you. Just don't hurt anyone." I wait to hear him confirm that he won't or that he hasn't, but he doesn't say any of those things.

Instead, he pushes the blade even further into my skin, and I can feel a trickle of blood running down the side of my neck. Tears fill my eyes as I beg him, "Please, Henry. Please tell me you didn't hurt him. Tell me you didn't kill Lucas."

He huffs with indignation. "He's not your concern anymore."

And then he begins to slowly drag me backwards with him, away from the farm.

Away from my home.

## CHAPTER 29

*Trinity*

HENRY HAD BEEN planning this for a while.

When we reach the front gate, I realize he has more weapons and a long rope stashed. He's quick to tie my wrists and waist with a length of rope left to use as a tether to keep me close on our journey…wherever we're going.

Once we're through the gate, he leads me through the woods with the rope in one hand and a large machete in the other.

I don't know where he got all the weapons or the rope, but I decide it doesn't matter. He hurt Lucas. I know he did. Perhaps even killed him. So, I make a vow that the first chance I get, I'm going to break free and go back to my home. And if I have to hurt Henry in the process, then so be it.

Henry walks in front of me with the rope taut between us. His head moves left to right as if it's on a swivel, looking this way and that, trying to spot creatures in the woods.

I look down at my bound wrists and notice the beaded necklace around my neck bouncing against my chest. If I break the cord and scatter the beads as a sort of crude bread crumb trail, Jack could track us. He was always making me look at bunny tracks and things in the woods, explaining that he could track them to their burrows. I'm sure if Jack sees the beads, he'd be able to follow our trail. That's a lot of *ifs*, but it's my only hope at this point.

With Henry's back towards me and his attention preoccupied, I decide this is the perfect opportunity. Reaching up with my bound hands, I grab hold of the necklace and pull. The string breaks and some beads fall down onto the forest floor, but I manage to gather most of the necklace in my palms, hiding the evidence.

Henry stops walking and turns. I'm so afraid I've been caught that I cease breathing altogether and just stand there like a deer in the headlights as he stares back at me.

"Did you hear something?" he asks.

"No," I say quickly. Maybe too quickly. But Henry doesn't seem to notice the change in my demeanor. "I kicked up a few rocks. Could that be what you heard?" I ask more calmly this time.

He huffs and then continues dragging me along by the rope.

"Where are we going, Henry?" I ask, masking the sound of the next bead I drop on the ground.

"Shh, be quiet!" he hisses, glancing all around us.

He's paranoid. Beyond paranoid. And he very well should be. We're in the woods alone where anything could get us.

We walk for what feels like hours, and I carefully drop bead after bead after bead until I only have two left. Tears fill my eyes as I realize my bread crumb trail is not going to work if we walk much farther.

But after a few more yards, Henry finally stops. "Honey, we're home," he says cheerfully, glancing back at me with that crazed look in his eyes.

I look up ahead where there's an old, abandoned hunting cabin deep in the woods with smoke billowing from the chimney.

Quickly, I throw my last bead to the forest floor, praying that the trail will lead Jack right to me.

And then I'm pulled towards my new home.

A home that's straight out of a nightmare.

## CHAPTER 30

*Carter*

IF I'VE LEARNED anything on this supply run, it's that I miss Trinity way more than I thought I would. I miss her smile, her laugh, her beautiful face.

And when I get back, I'm going to tell her as much.

Next time the guys decide to go on a supply run, I'll be the one that stays behind. There's nothing out here for me in this world anymore. Not when I have a beautiful angel like Trinity waiting at home for me.

I'm so distracted in my thoughts that it takes a moment for my brain to register the chorus of growls coming from the hallway of the library we're currently in.

"Fuck," I hiss angrily.

I told Owen it was risky to go into such a huge, open space like this, but he insisted. We hit the grocery store and pharmacy first and saved the library for last. Most of the places were ransacked, with zombies dead on the ground, but the library remained untouched. And now I know how stupid it was to come here.

Whistling low and loud for the other guys, I make my way

towards the exit. But when I'm almost out the door, I see Owen above me on the second floor, frantically searching for something.

"Owen," I whisper-yell.

The fucker acts like he doesn't even hear me, and it pisses me off.

The growls are getting louder and closer, and our opportunity for escape is rapidly closing in on us.

There could be three zombies. There could be seven…or fifteen. I mean, who the fuck knows at this point.

Jack is by my side in the next few seconds, and he's looking wearily up at Owen, who is still searching the bookshelves.

"Fuck, what is he doing?" I hiss.

Jack shakes his head in response and unsnaps his knives from his cargo pants, readying himself for a battle.

Cursing mentally to myself, I pull a long sword from its sheath situated on my back. I stole the damn thing from an abandoned museum several months back, and it's bad-ass. "Fuck it. I've been waiting to use this," I tell Jack with a grin.

He rolls his eyes and says, "Let's go get him before it's too late."

Armed with our weapons, we haul ass up to the second floor and straight to Owen. He's so focused on the books in front of him that he doesn't even see the zombie rounding the corner.

Knowing we wouldn't reach him in time, Jack pulls out his gun, aims and shoots the fucker in the head.

The sound echoes through the large library, and it sounds like a fucking cannon going off.

"Fuck," he barks angrily. "Anything within a one-mile radius is going to be coming for us now."

"Owen!" I grab him by the scruff of his shirt and haul his ass backwards. Clutched in his hands as if it's the most precious thing in the world is a copy of… "*Sense and Sensibility?*" I ask incredulously. "You're going to get us killed over fucking *Sense and Sensibility?*" I spit at him.

"Trinity wanted to add it to our library," he says in defense.

Rolling my eyes, I growl, "All right. Let's go, Romeo."

We take the stairs two, three, four at a time, bounding down them as fast as we can go. The zombies are just coming around the corner.

Jack stabs a few through the head as I swing my long sword, severing one almost in half.

"Holy shit!" I say in total awe. "This thing is totally bad-ass."

"Let's go," Jack growls in annoyance.

We leave through the front doors, narrowly making our escape. Not wanting to waste any more time in this town, we go straight to the truck chocked full of supplies and get the hell out of Dodge.

As we ride towards home with the windows down and music softly playing on the radio, I can't help but chuckle at the fact that Owen risked his life for a fucking book just because Trinity wanted it.

And then I think of the lengths I would go for her, and I suddenly understand him risking his life over a fucking *book*. Because when Trinity sees it, the smile on her face will have made it all worth it and then some.

It's in that moment that I realize that we're all fucked when it comes to that girl.

Head over heels kind of fucked.

## CHAPTER 31

*Jack*

THE MOMENT I park the truck, I know something's wrong. Usually Lucas hears the truck coming and opens the gate for us. Usually he's vigilant, ready with a gun just in case it's not us returning, but some outsider. This time he wasn't waiting by the gate, and he's not waiting on the front porch either.

I exchange a look with Carter, and the expression on his face tells me he's worried too.

Quickly, we get out of the truck, leaving behind all the supplies we just spent all day gathering and run towards the house.

But halfway there, I find out why Lucas didn't greet us at the gate.

His prone body is lying unmoving in the grass in front of the barn that holds the animals. I can smell the blood before I see it when I approach him. Kneeling down, I put my fingers to his neck and wait to feel a pulse.

Carter and Owen wait expectantly.

When I nod that he's still alive, they both release a collective sigh of relief.

I spot a shovel nearby covered in blood. "Someone hit him in the head with this," I explain.

Carter's eyes go wide when he asks, "Where's Trinity?"

Before I can even stem to guess, he's running towards the garden screaming her name while Owen takes off for the house. While they look for her, I tend to Lucas.

The nasty wound on the back of his head will need to be taken care of first before we do anything else. So, I gather him up in my arms and carry him inside.

Owen comes skidding to a stop in the kitchen, shaking his head with a sad look on his face.

*He didn't find her.*

Carter comes rushing into the house as I lay Lucas face down on the big farm table. "I can't find her anywhere," he says in a panic. "She's gone. Someone took her."

That's the conclusion I reached minutes ago. Someone came to the farm, put Lucas out of commission and kidnapped our girl.

"Owen, get Lucas's medical bag from his room. I need to bandage his head before we leave."

"Leave?" Carter asks as Owen races up the stairs, taking a few at a time.

"We're going to go find our girl," I tell him vehemently with anger coursing through my veins. "And we're going to *kill* whoever took her from us."

## CHAPTER 32

*Carter*

JACK IS A great tracker. He tracks small game, large game, humans — hell, even zombies.

So when he tells us that Trinity was in a struggle with someone near the garden, my stomach sinks.

Owen and I are helpless as we follow Jack after loading up on weapons.

*He's going to find her,* I keep telling myself. *This is what he does. He finds things.*

Jack leads us through the front gate and into the woods. He looks left and then right, not sure which way to go. "We'll try this way first," he tells us. "I'm pretty sure their tracks are leading this way."

*Pretty sure?* I want to say, but I keep my mouth shut. If I learned anything over the time I've gotten to know Jack, it's that you never second-guess the dude. He knows his stuff.

We follow him for a while until he stops. Owen crashes right into his gigantic back, and I try to stifle a laugh but fail miserably. Owen flashes me a pissed off look, and I simply shrug. I can't help it. That shit was funny.

Jack glares at both of us before bending down and picking up one of several beads lying on the forest floor. "These are from Trinity's necklace. I remember watching her make it the other day."

I stare at the tiny bead in his large palm and nod my head in agreement.

"Our little bird left us a trail of breadcrumbs to follow," Jack says with a wry grin.

The three of us continue on, spotting bead after bead every several feet. Our girl was smart to leave the beads since they'll hopefully lead us right to her. But fuck, whoever took her really went far into the woods. It's beyond where I've ever been, and even Jack said he doesn't venture this far.

Because it's too dangerous.

And my biggest fear is that we'll come up on Trinity's dead body, half eaten by the zombies that roam these woods.

It's getting dark, and I worry that we won't find her in time. There's no way I'm turning back now, however. I'll stay out here all night if I have to, and I know Jack and Owen would feel exactly the same way.

When we come to the last bead, Jack points off into the distance. There is a cabin with dim light spilling from the broken windows.

"Get ready, gentlemen. This might get messy," Jack says assertively.

## CHAPTER 33

*Trinity*

HENRY FILLS ME in on exactly what happened when we were separated. As I was ensnared in the trap that Jack had set for larger game, Henry had led the zombie away from me. He makes the whole thing seem heroic as if he saved my life or something.

He ended up stabbing the creature in the head with a pointed stick that he found. And after walking a while, he stumbled upon this abandoned hunting cabin. It was stocked with expired canned goods, and he used a barrel to collect rainwater to drink. He'd been surviving on his own, not leaving the cabin for weeks.

"And then, one day, I went back to see if I could find you," he explains, continuing on with his tale. "And I saw you. On the farm. In the barn. With *them*," he says with disgust.

I pull at the ropes that are currently wrapped around me, keeping me bound to the chair I'm currently sitting in. Night is beginning to fall outside the broken windows, and I fear that I won't make it out of this cabin alive.

"I was there that night," he says with a mischievous grin on his face. "I watched you fucking all of them." He sits back in his chair, rubbing at his scraggly, long beard. "I never pegged you for an orgy type of girl, Trinity." His words disgust me, and I turn to stare at the wall. "If I had known what a slut you were back when you were my employee, I would have called you into my office and bent you over my desk when I had the chance."

I cringe, biting my lower lip to hold back all the things I want to say to him. I want to tell him that I would have never slept with him even if he would have paid me a million dollars back then, but I keep my mouth shut.

Henry leans forward in his chair, placing his chin on his propped up hands. "They really had their way with you that night. I jacked off three times watching that shit."

My lips curl in disgust.

"Oh, don't act all high and mighty," he admonishes me. "I know what you are now, Trinity. You're a little whore."

Shaking my head, I scoff at him. He has no idea what those men truly mean to me. They're not just random hookups. My panties didn't automatically fall the first night I was in their house. I learned to love each one of them individually and honestly couldn't choose between them even if I had to. I love all of them equally.

I just wish I could have told them that before Henry kidnapped me. Knowing that my true, undying feelings might go forever unsaid has me hanging my head in agony and sadness.

"Aww, what's wrong, Trinity? Worried that your pussy won't get overused anymore?" he sneers. Standing, he walks closer to me, sending off alarm bells in my head. "Don't worry. I'll use you harder and more often than they ever did. I'll make you forget all about them. It will be as if they never existed." His dirty fingers reach for my face, pinching my jaw painfully and forcing me to look at him. "Maybe we should start right now. I want to see just how good that whore mouth of yours feels on my cock."

When he gets closer, I spit right in his face. He's stunned at first, taking a step back to wipe off the spittle from his cheek. And then a crazed, manic laugh escapes his mouth as he cackles, the sound echoing off the walls of the cabin.

"You're gonna pay for that, bitch," he hisses.

I don't even have time to react or brace for the impact when his fist connects with my cheek. My head whips to the side, stars forming behind my closed eyelids. The pain is intense, and it takes me a moment to recover.

I'm already dehydrated and hungry from the long hike in the woods. I was running on pure adrenaline before, but now I'm gassing out, running on fumes.

When I hear the sound of his belt jangling, my eyes snap open. He's standing before me, unzipping his jeans.

Squeezing my eyes shut, I shake my head rapidly, praying for some kind of a miracle.

"Open your mouth," he forces out. "Don't make me hurt you again, Trinity."

My lips stay clamped shut as I sob silently in the chair. I'm not going to make this easy on him. I'll never give in willingly.

He pulls his hand back to hit me again, but the door bursts open.

I scream loudly, thinking that the creatures in the woods found us. But when I see Jack standing in the doorway, the huge mountain of a man with a fierce look in his dark eyes, my scream instantly dies in my throat and turns into a relieved sob.

Henry scrambles for one of the weapons laid out on the table nearby, but Jack is too fast. Jack strides across the room and plunges a knife straight into Henry's hand, effectively pinning him to the table. Henry cries out in pain in a gut-wrenching scream.

Carter and Owen rush in and are quick to start untying me.

"Fancy meeting you here," Carter jokes with a wink, but I can see the worry and fear behind his green eyes. He was worried they wouldn't find me alive, and I was worried I would never see them again.

I weep in relief as I'm finally freed from the ropes and collapse into Carter's arms. He holds me tightly, shushing me.

The three of them gather around me, telling me that everything is going to be okay.

Peering over Carter's shoulder, I watch in horror as Henry grips the handle of the knife and pulls up, freeing his hand from the table. In the next second, he's charging towards Jack's turned back with the knife in his good hand.

"Jack!" I cry out.

With the quickest reflexes I've ever seen in a human, Jack turns and deflects Henry's attack. And then Jack comes up with a blade in his other hand, slicing across Henry's throat in one slick move.

Blood begins spraying from the wound as Henry collapses to the cabin floor. His mouth moves, but only a gurgling sound comes out, but I know he's saying my name as his eyes lock on me.

Gasping, I shield my eyes against Carter's chest against what will undoubtedly haunt my dreams at night.

"I'll take care of him," Jack tells us. "Get Trinity out of here."

I willingly allow Carter to guide me out of the cabin. When we're at a safe distance, I look up at Owen and ask, "Lucas…is he…?"

"He's okay," he assures me.

I almost collapse in relief, but Carter is there to keep me upright in his big, warm arms. He gently squeezes me a little harder as if he can't get me close enough. "I love you, Trinity," Carter says suddenly, and I can tell by his tone that he's wanted to tell me that for a long time.

This whole near-death experience has affected all of us. They were afraid to lose me, but I was even more scared to lose all of them. "I love you too," I whisper to him. And then I look over at Owen, who walks over to sandwich me between him and Carter. "I love you too, Owen."

"I love you. So much," he whispers, kissing my temple before resting his head against mine as he breathes softly into my hair.

Jack finally emerges from the darkness. He has a grim look on his face as he gives Carter a nod that it's done; but as soon as he sees me, his features soften. "Trinity," he rasps out.

He pulls me into his arms and holds me tightly as if I'm his whole world. Pulling back a little, I look up into his rugged face and tell him, "Jack, I love you."

"Fuck, I needed to hear that right now." He cups my face in his large palms and gives me a gentle kiss, so different from his usual kisses. "I love you more than anything in this fucking world, Trinity." He pulls me tighter against him, and I love the feeling of being in his big arms. "I would have moved heaven and earth to get you back. I'll never let anything happen to you ever again."

It's crazy to think I could love so many men at the same time, but the heart wants what it wants. And it wants all four of them locked up so tightly inside that nothing will ever come between us again.

Jack holds me for several long minutes, and then finally says quietly, "Let's get our girl home."

And it fills me up with so much joy that I openly weep at his words.

## CHAPTER 34

*Lucas*

MY HEAD IS pounding with a ferocity I've never experienced before. And when I hear voices and then footsteps bounding up the steps, it sets my senses all out of whack, causing me to lean over and puke into the bucket Jack thankfully left by my bedside.

When I'm done hurling, I slowly sit back up and see a large group of people at the foot of my bed. I blink my eyes, clearing my double vision before my eyes widen.

Trinity, Owen, Jack and Carter all stand there staring at me with worried looks on their faces.

"Am I...am I dreaming?" I ask. The pain pills I took earlier might still be affecting my mind. Hell, I thought I saw Santa Claus *and* the fucking Easter Bunny after I took them.

"If you're dreaming, then why the hell would *I* be in it?" Carter pipes up.

His smartass comment makes me smile. "You're right." I grimace as another pain shoots through my skull. "How did you...find her?"

Jack smiles proudly down at Trinity. "Our girl left me a trail in the forest. It was easy to track her right to the cabin that sonofabitch had her locked up in."

Trinity steps forward and gingerly sits on the bed beside me. Her cool hands press against my cheeks, bringing me back to reality. "How are you feeling?" she asks, concern lacing her voice.

"Like I got hit by a truck," I admit. And then I give her what I hope is a devilishly handsome smile before adding, "But I feel better now that you're here. I'm so glad you're home."

When my eyes finally begin to focus on her beautiful face, they instantly go to the bruise on her cheek. "He hurt you," I say through clenched teeth. "Fuck, I'll kill him."

"Already taken care of," Jack says with a pointed look towards me.

"Good," I reply coolly. I'm glad the bastard's dead. He had no right to come onto our land, no right to hit our girl and no right to take what's ours.

I pull Trinity into my arms and breathe in her scent, not ever wanting to let her out of my sight again.

"You gonna be okay?" she whispers into my ear.

I give her a small nod against her neck. "I have a concussion, but I'll recover. I'll be fine in no time. Just need some rest."

She pulls back and stares into my eyes with tears threatening to fall from hers. "I thought he killed you," she says, her voice breaking.

"I'm right here," I tell her, pulling her back into my arms. "I'll always be here. I'll never leave you. And I'll never let you go."

Carter clears his throat and rubs the back of his neck as he says, "I'll go fix something to eat. I'm sure we could all use something in our bellies."

I give him a nod and watch as he and the other two guys walk out of the room, giving Trinity and me some much needed alone time.

"I'm sorry I couldn't stop him," I tell her. "He caught me from behind, and I didn't even have a chance to defend myself."

"It's not your fault. Don't blame yourself," she says with a shake of her head. "Lucas, there's something I need to tell you," Trinity tells me before pulling back again. I miss her soothing warmth already. "When I thought I would never see you again, it's all I could think about.

How I would never be able to tell you the words I've been holding back." She takes my hands in hers and gazes into my eyes as she says, "Lucas, I love you. I'm so totally and completely in love with you."

Her words make my heart skip a beat inside of my chest. Fuck, I've been waiting for what feels like forever to hear those words come from her mouth. "Trinity, I love you too," I whisper. "More than I ever thought possible."

Lying back, I pull her down with me, and we lie in a comfortable silence on the bed together. I lazily stroke her hair as she draws pictures with her fingertips on my bare chest.

"It's so good to have you home," I whisper in her hair.

"It's good to be home," she whispers back.

And I close my eyes and savor this moment, because I feel like the luckiest damn bastard in the universe right now.

Even though the whole world around us turned to absolute shit, I found someone so very damn special to me.

And I wouldn't trade her for anything in this screwed up realm we're living in.

# EPILOGUE

*Trinity*

*Eight months later...*

I LOUNGE BACK on the couch as I watch Lucas, Jack, Owen and Carter decorate the Christmas tree in the corner of the living room. It's hard to believe the holiday is just around the corner. It feels like forever since I celebrated *any* holiday, let alone my all-time favorite one.

Lucas takes a break from decorating to come sit next to me on the couch. He gives me his signature sexy grin, and it instantly fills me with a warm, fuzzy feeling.

He snuggles me against his chest and kisses the top of my head, breathing in my scent, like he always does. I close my eyes for a moment, relishing in the sounds of the fire crackling in the nearby fireplace and the guys arguing over which ornament should go where and who gets to put the star on top.

Our tree is from the backyard, and we found the ornaments in the attic. They are old, maybe even considered antique, with lots of signs of wear and tear from over the years they were lovingly used by the family who owned this big farmhouse. And I think they're absolutely perfect.

Lucas gently runs his hand over my rounded belly, and my eyes instantly open as a smile forms on my face. This is our routine every night. I know he's making sure the baby is okay, still moving around and kicking, but also giving us something to bond over at the same time.

We think the baby is his, but we can't be sure obviously. However, we decided a long time ago that it doesn't really matter, because everyone will love the baby equally no matter what.

"I wonder if it will be a boy or a girl," he wonders aloud.

"Doesn't matter. I just hope he or she is healthy," I respond.

We're estimating I'm about six months pregnant. And while I'm both excited and scared all at the same time most days, I know this baby will be loved unconditionally. And that's more than I could ever ask for.

Our little one will be welcomed into the world by not one but four wonderful fathers and a mother who will love him or her more than anything.

My guys have been collecting everything baby related for the past few months now. They managed to find an abandoned baby store on one of their supply runs, and it's been a godsend. I have everything I need...and probably even stuff I don't.

We turned one of the spare bedrooms into a nursery, even painting the walls a nice, neutral yellow. The room is complete with a crib, a rocking chair, a white dresser...and a giant stuffed sloth that Carter insisted on getting during one of the supply runs, much to Jack's dismay.

I'm not sure the baby actually needs a giant sloth, but it is adorable, nonetheless.

A couple of years ago, I would have been terrified to bring a baby into a world like the one we are in now. But things have been slowly changing...for the better.

The zombies are being killed off, and the government is gradually gaining control once again. We're hopeful that someday our son or daughter will be able to go to a real school and have real friends and be able to travel the world and have his or her own adventures.

There are a lot of *ifs* and speculation, but it's nice to dream.

Right now we just have to take it one day at a time.

Lucas whispers that he has a surprise for me before standing and walking out of the room. A few minutes later, he returns with a tiny stocking that he hangs on a hook next to the five bigger ones already hanging on the mantle above the fireplace.

Tears fill my eyes as I stare at the tiny stocking and everything it represents.

I had a terrible childhood, and I never had a holiday where I didn't spend the day longing and wishing for a new family, one that loved me and took care of me and wanted to keep me. Forever.

It looks like my wish finally came true.

And our baby will have the family I always dreamed of and hoped for. And that makes my heart swell with so much joy that I feel overwhelmed with emotion.

*Cue the waterworks.*

Even though I have the biggest smile on my face, tears run down my face in rivulets.

Lucas, with a concerned look on his face, rushes over to me. "What's wrong, Trin?"

"Nothing," I tell him. "Everything is...perfect."

"Then why are you crying?" he asks with a crooked smile.

"Because I'm so happy."

Carter, Owen and Jack join us then, and my four men surround me in a circle. I can feel the love they have for me radiating off of them in waves, and it makes me almost break down again. But I suck it up and refuse to cry anymore, even if it is happy tears.

I look around at my four rough, rugged and wild men.

All so handsome.

And all so different.

They breathed new life into me when I thought I was ready to breathe my last.

And if I had to do it all over again, I wouldn't change a thing. Because for the first time in my life, I have a *real* family.

And it feels so damn good to love and be loved in return.

## THE END

## ACKNOWLEDGMENTS

Thank you to my ARC and beta readers. I couldn't do this without your time and support.
Thank you for your encouragement and for always believing in me.

## ABOUT THE AUTHOR

Thank you for reading! If you enjoyed reading *Claiming Her*, please consider telling your friends and posting a short review on Amazon. Word of mouth is an author's best friend and much appreciated. Shouts from rooftops are great too.

You can find all of my books exclusively on Amazon and free for Kindle Unlimited subscribers: http://amazon.com/author/angelasnyder

And please sign up for my newsletter to be notified of all of my new releases, giveaways, sneak peeks, freebies and more: http://eepurl.com/cNF0o5

## ALSO BY A.J. SNYDER

If you enjoyed reading Claiming Her, please check out my newest reverse harem, **Wrecked**.

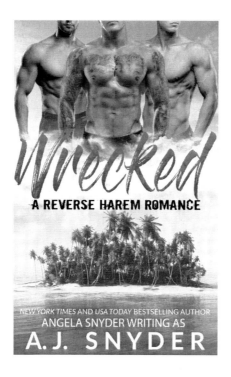

After a year of isolation, Gunner, Finn and Jamison never expected to be rescued.

And they certainly never expected a beautiful woman to crash land into their lonely existence.

Rose is the only ray of light in their dark storm, and they'll do anything to protect her.

But can the four of them survive without becoming completely wrecked?

Get your copy of **Wrecked** on Amazon here: https://viewbook.at/Wrecked